MAHJONG

MURDER

Elgin Lee

PARTRIDGE

A Penguin Random House Company

To order additional copies of this book, contact
Toll Free 800 101 2657 (Singapore)
Toll Free 1 800 81 7340 (Malaysia)
orders.singapore@partridgepublishing.com

www.partridgepublishing.com/singapore

Contents

At The Beans Café 1

Agnes Farell 5

Emily Mulshot 14

At The Blue Chip 20

Gina Farell 27

Bobby 41

Axel 55

Dr. Marion 69

Alvin Farell 82

James & Audrey Tholson 93

Dinner With The Farells 110

Mr. Buckling 121

Debbrah Rikers & Evelyn Flannel 125

The Calm Before The Storm 131

Revelation 137

Acknowledgements

I would like to say a very big thank you to my parents who supported my book project all the way and to those friends of mine who encouraged me, especially to Matheus who inspired the front cover design. I would also like to say many thanks to Mr. Fergus Brennan, whose guidance throughout the years is much appreciated. And, of course, none of this would be possible without God, through whom all things are done. Once more, thank you!

Prologue

"**P**hone call for you, sir," said Amy Bridgetts, her voice echoing through the relatively unfurnished hallways of Pekadin Mansion.

"Yes, thank you," said my long-time friend and world-renown detective Andrew Sommers as he picked up the receiver and positioned it gracefully at his right ear.

I sat across him, sipping my white coffee, slightly annoyed that at the most interesting point in our conversation regarding the unknown yet certain link between mankind and animals, Andrew had to answer the phone. After he was finished with the phone business, I would have lost my place and simply must stop there for it would be too irritating, even for me, to begin again. What a shame.

Then, my thoughts were diverted towards Andrew's increasingly urgent voice. Actually, his tone didn't change much, but forty years of friendship with him taught me many things. From what I could hear, I knew it was important.

Eventually, Andrew put the receiver down. I was a little jumpy and excited, but refused to sound desperate, so I started, "You really should have placed Amy in the adjacent room. I mean to say I pity her every time you get a phone call. What kind of secretary has to shout down the hallway just to get her boss's attention?" To emphasize my point, I made a clucking noise, followed by rolling my eyeballs.

But as we already know, I couldn't be bothered where Amy worked, so, without waiting for an answer, I proceeded with "What was that phone call about anyway?"

"I'm glad you should ask. Miss Agnes Farell from Little Flattington has just called me regarding a rather interesting murder case. She said her aunt was poisoned Friday two weeks ago and she would really like us to assist in the investigations. Seems the police aren't getting anywhere with that . . . ." said Andrew as calmly as ever. I couldn't believe my ears. To Andrew, these sort of phone calls were probably ordinary by now. But to me, this was exciting!

"What else did she say?"

"She said she hoped I will accept this case and if I did, to meet her tomorrow at The Beans Café. She will provide us with further details then."

"Well, are you accepting the case?"

"Of course; it will be like Sudoku, a mind-challenging puzzle," he said smugly. "I will enjoy solving it. Come along won't you?"

I was still laughing inside my mind over how he could accept cases like this purely for the fun of it and not, instead, for the responsibility of seeking justice when I agreed, my insides shaking like jelly. I had always wanted to watch the famous Andrew Sommers in action and thought it not possible in this lifetime of mine because he was actually semi-retired. But who can blame him at his age? Even great thinkers have to, well, *stop* thinking after a while . . . .

I went home that night very pleased with myself, very pleased indeed. Well, the animal subject would just have to wait.

At The Beans Café

T he next day, at The Beans Café, Andrew and I met Miss Agnes Farell for the first time, sitting at a little corner table, stirrer in hand, eyes staring out into nothingness. Her black dress matched her hair and shoes, all jet black, and also the surrounding ambience. Already a sense of mystery and deep sorrow blanketed her.

Andrew approached her very quietly and addressed her. She was startled, spilling some hot chocolate on the linen table cloth. But she adapted herself very quickly, and shook Andrew's hand, releasing a sigh of relief. "You're here at last," her eyes seemed to whisper.

So, we took our places, and I introduced myself as Andrew's assistant. In doing so, I took the opportunity to observe her body language, for anything 'extra' that her face could reveal. She had very soft eyes and fair skin and her lips were glossy with a shade of red lipstick. Rosewood I think. No other makeup, except for some powder. Definitely no mascara. Too innocent, but if I was looking for ways to hold her guilty by her looks, I would have failed.

"All right, if I may start?" she asked, when all three of us had hot drinks in front of us. Andrew nodded. I drooled with excitement, but in my mind only.

"As I've already told you, my aunt, Geraldine Stevenson, was poisoned on Friday night the 8th. She was playing mahjong with three others. One was her sister, that is to say, my mother, and two other guests: Evelyn Flannel and Debbrah Rikers. We consider them to be our neighbours although they live a few roads away. During the game, they had refreshments and it was discovered later that there was poison in my aunt's drink. She passed away during the course of that night, and it was the maid who found her dead the next morning."

She took a pause then continued:

"The police suspect murder and the autopsy confirmed that she was poisoned only a week later. We've been hounded endlessly by the police, and after a while, the questions get repeated and it's just stupid really. But the family is breaking apart and all of us are under severe stress and together with the heartache and grief, it's becoming unbearable. My sister's planning to move off with her husband and, and—that's why we all decided to get your help. We simply cannot stand this anymore. I know I haven't quite expressed myself as well as I had hoped, and it sounds really muddled up, but these *are* confusing times, and now, every day, we all stare at each other as if one of us has done it, and it most probably is the case. You see, we all don't believe she would have committed suicide. She had her fair share of health problems but that's normal for a seventy-one-year-old woman, and she was so *alive*, so to speak. But the other alternative is unthinkable. I've had nightmares these few days and life is so difficult for all of us. You do understand, I trust?" She finally stopped, tears swelling up in her eyes.

"Of course," said Andrew, offering her a piece of facial tissue. She took it, but merely crumpled it in her fist. The tears had subsided; she was a woman of strong character.

When things had calmed down a little, Andrew said, "It wouldn't be a problem if we were to pay you a visit some time, say, maybe this Saturday when everybody's home?"

"Yes, it's fine," she said.

"But first, I need to know who was in the house that night, and you need to be exact. Can you manage that?" The same gentle look met Andrew's kind gaze once more.

"Yes, let's see. I was home, and my aunt and mother of course, and there was Debbrah and Evelyn, Audrey, my sister, James, her husband, and their son, Bobby, and my brother Alvin. Wait, there was also Axel Lim.

He's a Hong Konger who is staying at our place with Bobby through a school student exchange program. He's supposed to have left some time ago, but after what happened, the police are retaining him for further investigations, but if you ask me, it' just stupid. He's quite obviously innocent and knows nothing about anything around here. And he's shaken up so much; he's not quite himself lately. Oh, yes, there was also our maid, Emily, who's been with us about a year now. That's about it I think.

"Very good. Today's Thursday. We'll see you in two day's time then?"

"Yes, I'll see you then. Once again, I thank you for helping us; we really need it now," she said, getting up very daintily, smiling at Andrew, then at me. "Till Saturday then."

When she had left, I nudged Andrew.

"Well what do you think?"

"I think that this will be an interesting case. A very interesting case indeed! The murder is in the family . . . ."

And we parted, me promising I'll meet him at 3 Charenpuff Road early Saturday morning.

Agnes Farell

The thirty-minute bus ride to Little Flattington was an enjoyable one. Despite living so near to the town, that was practically the first time I visited it. Too boring I suppose. Other than this case, I couldn't possibly imagine why I would want to be here, let alone live here.

When I arrived at the given address, Andrew was there already, apparently waiting for me. It was nine in the morning, we had both taken breakfast; it was time to work. I felt so excited, but I tried hard to control myself. After all, Andrew Sommer's assistant needed to maintain a certain standard, I thought as I chuckled to myself.

So, we knocked at the front door, and not too long afterward, the butler greeted us and let us in with a simple, "Miss Farell is waiting for you in the living room," as he led the way. The house was very modern, with matching wooden furniture arranged artistically at the entrance and along the hallways. The vintage lights were not switched on, and although the curtains were drawn, the house was dark and gloomy. In that aspect, the house was ancient looking I suppose. Just before we entered the living room, the butler remembered to ask us for our coats and hats, then hung them in the coat stand where we entered. Old, but inexperienced, I thought to myself.

Agnes was wearing another black dress, distinctly different from the last one, but no less depressing. Again, her sweet smile greeted us, and she began by saying, "Shall we take this to the study?"

"Anything that pleases you, madam," Andrew said.

"Please, call me Agnes."

An awkward time for that, but I suppose she was too flabbergasted in the café that day to afford that cool luxury.

We continued along the hallway, decorated with various original paintings, to the adjacent room. The study was well furnished too, and it was somewhat less gloomy in here. The shelves were graced with an assortment of very sophisticated books, from dictionaries to novels. I had a quick glance and I caught sight of a copy of 'The Great Gatsby', 'A Tale of Two Cities' and 'Computing Skills for Dummies'. I must make it a point to borrow that last book. But later.

We were seated in comfy armchairs, near the electric heaters and a lamp stand. Agnes herself passed us some cushions from a closet and took her seat.

"I'm afraid I'm among the only ones who are in this morning. You see, Audrey and James went to the market to buy some things, Bobby and Axel went to play tennis at the local sports club, Alvin's somewhere having late breakfast, and the cook's having her coffee break. My mother's in sleeping because she had some medication last night that puts her right out, for a long time too, and Emily, our maid, you remember don't you, is also somewhere around the house. You've obviously met Sebastian, the butler, and here I am. I did tell everybody you'd be here, but still . . . ." She shrugged apologetically, then smiled again.

"That's not a problem, Agnes," said Andrew. "We can get started first while waiting for the others to come back. First, give me your account of what happened that night."

"Well, it was Friday the 8th, and we were all having dinner in the dining room, even Axel, Debbrah and Evelyn. You see, it's quite usual for Debbrah and Evelyn to drop by and spend the evening with my aunt, and that's a good thing too, because they keep each other such good company. That was about seven thirty and I think we finished at around eight fifteen, where everybody kind of just went their own ways. I think Bobby and Axel went to their room, and so did Audrey and James. Alvin left the house to buy some cigarettes at the drugstore, just five minute's walk from here. Sebastian and our cook, Betty had already left by then. Sebastian leaves at about six in the evening everyday and Betty leaves at around seven, after she's cooked dinner. Then, around seven thirty, Emily serves dinner, but she stays here and has her own room. So, anyway, after dinner, Emily cleared the table and helped set up the mahjong table, upon which the game began. Geraldine, Gina, Debbrah and Evelyn played, no one else is interested or even knows how to play I think, except for Axel. You see, it's quite interesting really, Axel stayed here a year ago as well through the same student exchange program and as a gift to the household, he presented the mahjong set, and of course taught us how to play. Like I said, none of us were interested, but my aunt fell head over heels over those silly little pieces and to make matters worse, she learnt soon enough that she could actually gamble small amounts of money with that game! Since then, she's been addicted and keeps pestering us to play with her, but we're all simply too busy. So, finally, she got Evelyn and Debbrah who are all suckers for the game, and my mother also. Well, I don't really care then. So long as they're happy and we're happy, everything's fine, right? At around nine, refreshments were served by Emily. I was with her, baking some cookies in the kitchen while she washed the dishes after dinner. I love baking by the way, and I was free that night, so I thought why not? The cookies were supposed to go with the coffee that Emily later served. And since I was in the kitchen, I actually watched Emily prepare the drinks, and she *didn't* put anything inside them. And, oh, it's just so dreadful, because you see, since I was actually there in the kitchen that night, everybody suspects me of, well, doing *it* but I can assure you Mr. Sommers that I *didn't* do it," she paused for effect, and what she said was with such force that it was hard for me to shake her words. She was telling the absolute truth. It was virtually impossible to imagine otherwise. I expected her to burst out crying at this point of time, but she clearly had no intentions to do so whatsoever. Her face hardened with a sort of resentment, probably thinking that this was a mistake after all, but I couldn't be sure. Andrew merely said, "Please continue."

"All of them had coffee that night. It was served in a pot, and they poured out the drinks themselves into individual cups as far as I know. The cookies were served as well, and I definitely didn't spike the batter in case you were wondering because I sampled one, and yet here I am, still alive!"

"No, I don't think the cookies were poisoned at all because then all four players would be dead, assuming they all ate the cookies."

"Yes, that was my point. Anyway, after the refreshments were served I went upstairs for a hot shower and then went into my room, picked up my storybook and read till about half past ten when I went to bed. The next thing I knew it was morning, and Geraldine had been found dead. Emily's screams woke everybody up at about seven thirty, and as you can see, nothing's quite been the same," said Agnes.

"All right, how did any of you know she was poisoned because of the coffee that night? It could have been something she had at dinner for example."

"According to my mother and the two guests, they all played till half past midnight; Emily would have gone to bed by then. That means that the cups and plates and mahjong pieces and whatever else would have been left till morning to be cleared up. That sort of thing happens quite often around here, I'm ashamed to say. Anyway, Emily normally wakes up at seven and wakes my aunt around seven thirty. It has to be early because she goes for brisk walking exercises at the park. Good for her body and all, but other than her, the rest of us sleep in till about nine latest. So what I mean to say is that Emily wakes her up first before attending to any of her chores, for example, clearing the table. But she found her dead, and naturally, nothing can be done about anything; she's all shaken up. Then, it's not until sometime later in the evening that the police, having already asked the basic questions and made many notes, confiscated the cups and pot and whatever else was left on the table, and on Monday, they told us there was poison, strychnine, in one of the cups, hers of course, but not in the pot. We have everything back with us now, but it's all been washed and so on. So, we know that's how she died," she finished.

"How did you know it was her cup for sure? Were they all identical or did hers have any special marking on it to distinguish it from the rest?"

"Well, they were all the same, and now that you mention it, we don't actually know for sure it was *her* cup that had the poison in it; we just assumed because, well, she's dead! And anyway, whose cup could it have been if it wasn't hers?"

"Ok, point taken. Next, what sort of person was your aunt?" Andrew asked.

"She's, well, she's a nice person. Typically moody and grouchy at times, but she does try to be nice. For example, she's let us all stay here until we're more stable with our income. The doctor says she's quite healthy, but in my opinion, she isn't. Her heart is weak and she's prone to minor heart attacks, but she takes the necessary medication. I suppose even a mild dose of any poison would have been fatal."

'That is unfortunate indeed. How is she financially?"

"She's very rich. This is her house. Left behind by her late husband. He was a doctor, a very popular one in the old days, but he died of liver failure, leaving behind a lot in his bank account. And she's a bit of a miser, who saves where she can and doesn't spend foolishly. Even her gambling is restricted to about two dollars a game and so on."

"Who would stand to gain from her death?"

"Her will? We don't know yet what is in it. It's currently with her lawyer, but I should think that all her money would be divided among my siblings and me, and of course my mother. The lawyer did call about a week ago to arrange a date and time when he could read her will out, but we were all distraught, what with the funeral having taken a lot out of us. You know how it's like; the funerals are always the worst, they're the final 'goodbyes', and anyway, we already had in mind getting outside help. We hadn't decided on, well, *you* exactly, but whatever form the 'help' would take, we decided to wait till it was over. So, after you've settled this matter, I'll ring Mr. Buckling up. Then, we'll know for sure.

"She doesn't donate to charity, I presume?"

"Knowing her, probably not, but I can't be sure."

'Ok, I think that will be all this morning. I can see you're quite tired already, but that's normal; anybody having gone through all you've gone through would be."

"Oh, it's quite alright; all of us are tired. The faster we finish this, the better. Is there anything else?"

"I might have more questions, but that can wait. For now, if I may have the contact number of Miss Stevenson's lawyer, and hopefully, her doctor as well, that would be of great help."

"Of course, let's see. Her lawyer is Mr. Buckling and her doctor, Dr. Marion. Here are their name cards," she said, passing us two separate cards which she produced from one of the table drawers.

"Thank you. And could we please have a word with Emily, your maid?"

Yes, I'll go tell her to come in. Thank you for coming this morning," she said. She was in complete control of herself, and the manner in which she glided out of the room impacted me severely. She seemed to bring all the mystery out with her, and now the study was as dull as ever.

"What do you think so far?" I asked Andrew.

"Ah, patience. It's too early for anything." He smiled at me. Emily walked in not long after.

Emily Mulshot

Emily was quite thin and short, about half a head shorter than me and she had long blonde hair which she tied into a ponytail with a piece of lilac-coloured hair band. She wore a uniform; typical, black sleeves and white body. She looked young, I would say around twenty-five, yet upon closer inspection, she looked older than Agnes, more haggard-looking. But that's all quite understandable; she's a maid and Agnes probably does face lifts and pedicures and manicures and who knows what else.

"Good morning, detectives," she said as she sat down.

"Good morning. First, we would like to know a bit about you. What's your full name?"

"My name is Emily Mulshot."

"Very well, where are you from?"

"I come from Mellowshire. It's a very small and poor town about two hours away from here by train. Most of the townsfolk are uneducated farmers; we have very good land you see, but my family is not so fortunate. I'm an only child, and both my parents are not fit to farm. It was by God's will that I came across a newspaper advertisement for domestic help here in Little Flattington. The pay is good; I send my parents some money by mail every month, and still have some nice leftovers for myself. My meals and accommodation are provided, and I need not be educated for this job!" she finished. She toiled with her hair at this point of time, smiling with satisfaction. "I am most thankful for this job."

I was surprised to see how quickly she had opened up. Her speech came quite naturally.

"How old are you and how long have you worked here?"

"I'm twenty-six this year, and I've been working here since April last year, so that's about one and half years."

"Perfect so far. Now, I want you to tell me what happened on the evening of the 8th of October."

"Oh, the 8th, that's the night she, um, died, right?" She was already quite uncomfortable.

"Yes."

"Well, to start with, all the members of the household were having dinner in the dining room; there was Madam Geraldine, Madam Gina, Agnes, Audrey, James, Alvin, Bobby and Axel. Also present were Miss Debbrah and Miss Evelyn. Let me see, nine, no, ten of them were at the table; yes, that's right. I trust Miss Agnes has already mentioned all of them to you?"

Andrew nodded.

"By dinner, Betty, the cook, and Sebastian, you know, the butler, had gone home. Betty lives two roads away and Sebastian has his own little flat somewhere, I'm not quite sure where, in town. So that leaves me. I was particularly busy that night, running to and fro between the kitchen and the dining room, meeting the requests of, well, everybody else. I remember distinctly Axel asking for a napkin, someone else wanted more ice in his drink, and another wanted a brandy refill, and the list goes on. I was so glad when the meal was over; I was just so exhausted. After clearing the table and setting the mahjong table up, I went into the kitchen and prepared the refreshments; all of them wanted to have coffee, so I boiled the water and waited for the coffee to brew. After it was ready, I served it in a pot together with four cups, oh, and Agnes' cookies as well, you do know she was baking that night, right?"

"Yes, Agnes told us she was with you in the kitchen the whole time."

"Yes, anyway, not too long after serving the coffee and cookies, I went to bed. I simply could not wait for them to finish playing."

"What time, precisely, did you go to bed?"

"I should think around half past nine, but I'm not sure."

"What about Agnes?"

"Well, her cookies were ready by eight fifty, so I think she tasted one of those Macedonian nut cookies and then left the kitchen. I didn't see her again that night. Wait, let me think. I know I'm forgetting to tell you something. Something important . . . . ooh, when I do remember, I'll be sure to inform you. I'm so sorry, detectives." She looked rather silly with that puzzled look on her face. "Is there anything else?"

"Yes, what do you think of Geraldine, your mistress, as a person?"

"Well, she treats me the way a boss should treat her worker. She says her 'please's and 'thank you's, but she berates me at times when I make mistakes, and she never buys me gifts or treats or things like that, not that I expect her to. The pay here is good enough."

"What mistakes do you actually make that warrant such berating or punishments?"

Emily took quite some time to think, then finally answered, "Well, um, maybe over things I damage or break sometimes. There was this expensive vase I broke by accident once, just elbowed off the hall table while dusting. She made a huge fuss over that, and she did deduct my salary that month, which I do deserve, but still I think it's a little wicked of her. It was an accident after all. I really can't remember any other such incidents, but there were also times when I left windows open when it was raining and misplaced a few things every now and then, but I always found them back! That really is all."

"One last thing: in light of recent happenings, are you planning to stay on here?"

"Yes, definitely, because I need the money to support my family. So, I hope they won't fire me or something like that. But they shouldn't since I really did not poison the mistress," she said forcefully.

"Don't worry. I'm sure they won't, unless they really do find you guilty," said Andrew, smiling. "That's all. Thank you for your time."

"It was my pleasure. I hope you succeed in finding out the truth. This really is terrible business, really terrible indeed," she said.

On our way out of, we met Agnes sitting in the living room, apparently waiting for us to be finished.

"Mr. Sommers, Mr. Philipps, I'm afraid there's simply no one else in who can meet you. Since it's nearly lunch time, why don't you two go grab a bite at, I recommend, The Blue Chip. They serve an excellent selection of western dishes and a range of unique concoctions at reasonable prices. It's just a few minutes' walk from here. Turn right from our front gate and keep walking straight. You can't miss it. I'd join you, but I have a luncheon with some other friends of mine. When you're finished, please do drop by and check if there's anyone free for you to question. It doesn't really matter whether I'm back or not by then because everybody knows your name and is expecting you. If you need me, do call me. You have my number, yes?"

"Yes, I do and your plan is fine. We'll drop by after lunch then. Don't hurry through your luncheon because of us," Andrew said, chuckling. His thick moustache was bobbing up and down as he spoke, a pretty interesting phenomenon to watch.

We shook hands with Agnes, and left the Stevenson Mansion.

At The Blue Chip

We walked further down, following closely the instructions that Agnes gave until at last, we arrived at The Blue Chip. I was so hungry and cold, and the wind kept blowing into my coat, chilling me faster than my internal heat energy was warming me. Andrew was, however, enjoying the breeze on his face and was a little reluctant to step into the warm and, according to him, stuffy interior of the posh restaurant.

But I wasn't taking no for an answer. I was dying of hunger and my stomach was grumbling; I wanted to eat . . . . *now*! Once inside, the aromatic and delectable scents coming from the kitchen invaded my nostrils, oh, I could smell black pepper sauce, mushroom soup, oil from the French fries; it was simply an amazing experience. I must have drooled, though for my sake, I hope not.

Upon closer inspection, the place was more like a pub: there was the drinks bar that was behind the bead curtain, and I could also see wooden tables and chairs opposite the bar from where I stood. A waiter, tall and slender, brought us to a table for two, and upon Andrew's request, a corner one for privacy. Well, he was a detective after all! That must have come naturally to him.

And the fact that we were here on important business, having conducted a couple of interrogations, placed particular importance on this meal. At least for me it did. Was Andrew going to quietly, secretively, proclaim that, oh, he, the great and wise detective, had deduced who the murderer was, given whatever little information he currently had in his hands? Was he going to explain his trend of thought for me to learn from? Not to mention, the gloomy nature of the day, the dim lights of the restaurant, everything—yes, privacy was certainly the pre-requisite!

A quick glance at the whole (small) restaurant showed me that there were a few individuals already eating, a family of three who had drinks on the table, but no food yet, and a couple who was holding menus in their hands who had quite obviously not ordered yet.

I sat opposite Andrew at a table in probably the darkest corner of the room, my hands fumbling with the menu. Hmmm, everything looked so delicious, and it took me a great deal of time before I decided on a bowl of mushroom soup (refillable), a portion of garlic bread, two honey-roasted chicken wings, and a large portion of fish and chips. Oh yes, I almost forgot: a double chocolate milkshake (this one was *not*, however, refillable, much to my regret). In stark contrast, Andrew had only ordered a small portion of chicken chop and a glass of diet coke.

"How do you eat so much?" he asked me sarcastically.

"And how do *you* manage with so little? Detective work is hard work; you should know that."

"Yes, but look here friend, I'm the only one who was asking questions the whole morning. And you? I'm not even sure if you absorbed half of what was said!"

"I *did* absorb everything," I said, sulking a little. "Anyway, the food isn't here yet. Start talking."

"About what?"

"Oh, come on! Don't tell me you don't know!"

"No, I don't," he said flatly.

I was getting seriously frustrated with him at that point of time; first, he invites me along on this 'adventure' with him, and now, not even half way through it, he's lost interest!

"The murder!" My voice was hoarse and came out barely audible. "The whole reason we're here in the first place!"

But Andrew only smiled, and I realized he was pulling my leg the whole time.

"Alright, alright. Don't be too excited, and keep your voice *down!*" He hissed that last word out. "Actually, I've a better idea. Since you said you heard everything and remembered everything, why don't you display your findings, and after you're done, I'll compare your theory with mine. Then, it'll be my turn to speak. That's a more interesting way of doing it, isn't it?"

Oops. My plan had backfired quite miserably. That was *not* how I planned things to turn out. I was reluctant to do that for two reasons: first, I heard everything, but I could hardly draw any conclusions from that little information, and second, Andrew might just laugh at how poorly I did the whole detective business. But seeing how adamant he was, I supposed I would have to try. Or face stone cold silence as the alternative. And so, I started, hoping desperately to be able to bluff my way through.

"So, what we know so far is that Emily and Agnes gave very similar accounts, so we have to assume for the time-being that what they said is the truth. Going by that, we know that it couldn't be the cook or the butler because they were not in, nor could it have been Alvin, who was out buying some cigarettes at the drugstore.

In my opinion, it couldn't have been Bobby or Axel because boys their age on a Friday night would be crazy with computer games. I suppose even if a bomb were to detonate right outside their doorstep, they wouldn't know it. Also, they would be each other's alibi."

I paused there, quite out of breath, but pleased with what I'd produced so far. Andrew nodded, a sign for me to continue.

"I also doubt, though I have no valid reason to, that Audrey and James were involved. I know we know close to nothing about them, but it's just a hunch I have. So, that leaves Agnes, Emily, Gina, Debbrah and Evelyn, with the first two being the prime suspects."

"Why?" Andrew asked, catching me off guard.

"Well, it's quite obvious, isn't it? They had the best chance to put the stuff in; Emily, especially, because she served the cups, meaning she could have very easily passed the cup with the poison to Geraldine. And I suppose, if anybody at the table had done it, the deceased would have noticed. Of course, there's the possibility of suicide, but I think that's not likely, because there were better ways to do oneself in. Why at a mahjong game? Next up is Geraldine's personality. Agnes describes her as nice, but miserly, and Emily isn't very pleased with the way she was petty over minor issues. This leads us on to motives. It would seem everybody present in the house that night would have motives for killing her, except Evelyn, Debbrah and

Axel who stand to gain nothing from her death. For the household members, the motive would be money, whereas for Emily, the motive would have been spite."

At this point, my soup and the drinks were served. I finished my bowl of soup in less than a minute, and quickly asked for a refill. While waiting, I continued:

"I'm almost done I'm afraid, but I do wonder what was so important that Emily forgot. I wish she'd remember; it would be of great help I suppose. Every little piece of information."

"You're right about almost everything, except for Alvin's part. You said he wasn't home when the poison was administered, but, according to Agnes, dinner finished around eight fifteen, upon which Alvin left home to buy some cigarettes. Yes. At the drugstore which is only *five minutes* away from the house. How long would it take one to buy cigarettes? Not very long. I think that he was home before nine, which makes him as likely a murderer as everybody else," said Andrew. "Also, you have no basis for marking anyone off and focusing solely on Agnes and Emily, although they do seem to be the most likely suspects. Funny how neither Emily nor Agnes brought up the topic of Alvin again after simply mentioning he had gone out. They didn't say anything about him coming back . . . ."

"Enough; it's your turn to tell me about your findings instead of just correcting me . . . ." I said smugly.

But as life would have it, the food, together with my soup refill, reached the table then. Sigh. His theory would have to wait for later, I thought as my hands grabbed the silver fork and knife. As desperate as I was to know what Andrew had deduced so far, my stomach had first priority.

Gina Farell

After lunch (if I had to add, superbly delicious), we took a leisurely stroll back to the mansion. Andrew said little, if not nothing, I didn't already know when I pressured him to keep his end of the bargain. I'm sure he was just copying what I said to please me. But no matter, sooner or later, he would have to tell me the truth.

It was no longer cloudy, and sunlight illuminated almost everything, so much so that I began to feel hot and sweaty. Nevertheless, I'd rather walk in that weather than in the unpleasant, blustery conditions of earlier that day.

Along the way, we found the drugstore Agnes referred to by its name: Smiths Drugstore Pte Ltd. Andrew turned to go in, and I followed blindly . . . . until he stopped dead in his tracks and I bumped into him.

"What's the matt—" I began, but ended in and 'Oh!' when I caught sight of a sign that read 'Out For Lunch. Back at 1.30pm". It was only one o'clock, so waiting would be foolish.

"We'll come back later," said Andrew.

So, once more, we knocked on the door to the Stevenson Mansion, and once more, Sebastian let us in, but this time, he remembered to ask us for our coats and hats immediately.

"Is Miss Agnes Farell home?" Andrew asked.

"No, she is not I'm afraid. Is there anybody else you would like to speak with?"

"Is Mrs. Gina Farell in then?"

"Yes, she is. Perhaps you would like to wait in the study while I inform her?"

"Perfect, thank you."

We made our way to the study and let ourselves in. The room was very bright, unlike this morning. And as we took our seats, I realized that even the cushions were left untouched, almost as if in anticipation of our return.

Soon (sooner than I expected), Gina Farell walked in. She was a woman in her sixties, and based on the photograph we had seen of Geraldine, I'd say they were definitely sisters. In particular, they had the same chin and facial bone structure; a long face that ended in a pointy chin, and all the other facial features just fell into place, and of course, at her age, the wrinkles had their say as well.

"Good afternoon," she said.

"Good afternoon. I hope you can spare us some time because I would like to ask a few questions regarding the unfortunate death of your sister."

"Yes, Agnes already told me you'd be visiting. Please, just start and get this over with." Her tone was a little less than polite.

"Alright then, how old are you, Mrs. Farell?"

"Sixty-five."

"That would make you six years younger than your sister, yes?"

"Just as you said."

"Tell me about your family history, and about your sister; what kind of person she was, and so on."

"We come from a very poor background, Mr. Sommers. My parents were both rubbish collectors in the town of North Samaria. We could only afford to rent a room in which we, my sister and I, spent all our childhood years in. And, needless to say, our room was very small and cramped. Still, looking back, those were the happiest days of my life."

She paused here and a tear drop rolled down her left cheek. I felt a little sad too, watching her sob.

"I'm so sorry," she continued. "It's just that these few days are, um, very depressing."

"It's quite alright. Just take your time," said Andrew.

"In our town, the rich are very rich, and the poor are very poor. But then again, probably everybody seemed rich to us at that point of time. I felt that we were among the poorest, if not the poorest, people in the town. For example, my parents used to collect rubbish from the houses of some of my classmates, none of us being the wiser. I had no friends, not because the others were snobbish; no, it was because I felt inferior and somehow it showed when I was around others, so, without meaning to, I chased them off. Geraldine didn't have any friends either, so all we had was each other, whether it was in school or anywhere else even thought we were six years apart. We were *that* close."

She paused again to compose herself, and upon realizing she had nothing left to say, Andrew continued.

"Do tell me, how did she move out of such poverty and end up here in a beautiful house like this? I understand that this *is* her house."

"After she graduated from high school, at around eighteen, a doctor from one of the neighbourhoods fell in love with her, and two years later, they got married quietly. I don't remember how old he was when that happened. It's not for me to say if she truly loved him, or if she was just desperate to find easy money. I know what I'm saying reflects poorly on her, but you must understand, after all we've been through, anybody would have done what she did as well. Her husband was a good man, and he supported my whole family. My parents didn't need to collect rubbish anymore, you see. And we even managed to rent a small house instead of just that one room. So, I suppose even if she didn't love him, she would have been obliged to marry him for the sake of all us. But within the next ten years, both my parents passed away because of health problems, and, oh, I don't want to go into the details of that if you don't mind. I just don't want to, and I don't quite see how that sort of information will help with this case—"

"It's quite alright; we don't need to know," said Andrew, cutting her off before she lost her temper. "Just stick to what you think is important."

"Yes, yes, ok. After my parents died, Geraldine simply insisted to move far away from home, saying things like 'there's nothing more left here for us except for death and sorrow', and Daniel was stable, making quite a lot of money, enough to buy this house, and after he too died, my sister found herself in sole possession of this house and whatever else was left in the bank account. I was happy for her because she was finally rich!" she said, ending in a triumphant note.

"How long have you lived here?"

"About thirty years I think. You see, originally, I stayed here with the couple when they first bought this place. Then, when I eventually got married, I moved off. But my husband wasn't rich, you see, so we could only afford to rent a flat. It was demolished a few years ago though, due to some flaw in the safety of the foundation, so I can't show you where it is now."

"Who is your husband? Nobody's mentioned anything about him."

"And indeed they haven't!" she said spitefully. "After my brother-in law died of liver failure, Geraldine was lonely, and so I offered to move in with her. And why not? I already had Alvin and Audrey with me, and the flat was getting a bit too crowded for all of us, and I thought maybe having children around would help lift Geraldine out of her grief. We were, after all, family. She may not have loved Daniel when he was alive, but after he died, the way she cried showed me how much she missed him. It wasn't all about the money; not the way I thought it was. She agreed, and so, we moved in and sold the flat off. For a while, everything was perfect! Merrick would go teach in the school, Alvin and Audrey would stay home with me and Geraldine. She was getting better; she really was. She seemed to be able to deal with Daniel's death better."

She took another pause as tears of nostalgia had set in.

"What happened next?"

"Then, I was pregnant; pregnant with Agnes. Then, oh, then one night, Merrick came home. He was drunk! He just burst into the dining room when we were having dinner. He was such a huge mess: his hair, his clothes, everything! But what came next was worse. He had a murderous look in his eyes and I knew he was going to do something drastic. And he did! He said, shouted rather, something about the baby and money and joy and comfort as long as we lived, and the next thing I know he had his hands around Geraldine's neck. He was strangling her! Of course, now, I know he did it for her money but he wasn't thinking straight! He wasn't himself! I mean even if he succeeded, he would never have gotten away with it. Anyway, I ordered Alvin and Audrey upstairs, and I myself tried to pull Merrick off her, but how could I when I was already five months pregnant? But when he felt me tugging at him, he shoved me and I hit the table edge on my side and screamed in pain. Merrick released Geraldine and turned his attention to the baby inside me and oh, everything happened so quickly! The next thing I remember was Geraldine; she had a knife in her hands and she had stabbed Merrick in his back! Then, one more time, in his chest this time, and he fell to the floor, and lay motionless. He was dead. Dead! My sister murdered my husband!" A pause, followed by: "But she didn't know what she was doing either; it was a completely instinctive move. Yet, she had killed him. It was too late for anything. The paramedics confirmed his death, and when the police gave their questions, I sided Geraldine. What else was there to do? My husband was dead, and Geraldine was still my sister in blood, who loved me and would provide for my children and me. But we were never the same again. But believe me when I say I'm not angry enough with her to have murdered her."

"I'm sorry to hear about what happened to your husband but rest assured, we are not suggesting anything yet," Andrew said calmly. "Tell us about your children."

"Oh, you mean Alvin? Or Audrey or Agnes?"

"All three if you can."

"Let's see. Alvin has a degree in accounting, and he graduated from King's Council University about ten years ago, when he was twenty-five. He was jobless for a year, then he found a job in London and moved there. He wrote to us regularly but never sent any money back. I didn't insist, of course, because we have enough to live on here. Then he came home a month ago, saying he had left his job. Stress or something like that. But I didn't ask him anymore on that. You can if you want to. I mean, you can ask him yourself."

"And Audrey?"

"Audrey? Audrey isn't a very bright child. She's thirty-four this year, a year younger than Alvin, and she never went to any university. But, luckily for her, she's attractive and James soon fell in love with her and how happy I was for her when I found out he was a medical student! You will forgive me for being so materialistic, won't you? The years have taught me a great deal. But I suppose they love each other very much, so it's fine. They married when she was nineteen, and he twenty-three, a few years from graduating. They met by chance, you see. James is from North Samaria as well, and I was excited because his parents were probably my schoolmates, and you know how it is. It's always nice to be able to, how do you say this, keep in touch with your old hometown and so on. Anyway, he came here during his semester break on a tour of a few towns, Little Flattington included, with a few of his friends. Audrey was walking along a street that day, I don't remember doing what; they met and had a little chat, and she offered to take them around town, and I guess they soon fell in love. They had their first son, Bobby, a few months after marriage, and well, Geraldine and I helped take care of her baby while James finished his course. He spent every holiday since then here in this house. And after graduation, he moved in and is now working in the general hospital in the heart of town."

"And lastly, Agnes?"

"Agnes has a degree in business studies. She's thirty and she graduated four years ago from the same university as Alvin. She hasn't found a job yet, and if you ask me, she's just lazy. So, she's been living here as well since graduation, supported by Geraldine also, of course."

Did I sense spite in her voice at that last bit? I don't know.

"Very good. Next, can you please give me your account of what happened on October 8th, perhaps starting from after dinner?"

"After dinner? Hmm . . . . mahjong. You already know that Evelyn and Debbrah were present, I assume?"

Andrew nodded.

"Emily helped us set up the mahjong table; then, she went into the kitchen. And soon, the game started. You know how it is with mahjong. Once you start, nothing else really seems to matter to you. I can say that I didn't observe or see anything that would be of much help to you. All I remember seeing were 'Bamboos' and 'Joker' tiles, and you understand the rest, I'm sure."

"When were the refreshments served?" I understand all four of you had coffee that night. Am I right?"

"Yes, we did. Emily brought the coffee out after about three rounds were over. I remember distinctly that Geraldine had won all three. All the right tiles went to her at the right times! Her luck was unusually good that night."

"Apparently not good enough to have saved her life . . . ." I thought to myself.

"May I ask a rather personal question? Why coffee? Was it a usual beverage to have here at such a time of the night?"

"Oh, no; not usual at all. We normally only have coffee on mahjong nights because we all need to stay awake for the game. On normal nights, we have tea instead."

"So, it's coffee for mahjong nights and tea otherwise?"

"Yes, you can put it like that. But why? What does this matter to you?"

"I'm afraid now's not the time to answer such questions, but rather to ask them. Anyway, could I have the time the coffee was served?"

"I think it was around eight fifty, closer to nine, perhaps."

"What time did you finish?" I mean to say, what time did you retire to bed?"

"We finished at half past midnight. Then, Geraldine went to bed and so did I. We have our separate rooms, you see. Eve and Deb went home. They, too, stay separately."

"Did Geraldine complain about anything that night? For example: stomach pains, headaches and so on?"

"No, she didn't. She was fairly quiet during the game, but I guess we all were. Mahjong is serious business to us, you know. She mentioned something about the coffee, but not about the taste, something like it was too cold or too coarse. I don't remember now. But none of us said anything because we didn't feel that way."

"Did anything out of the ordinary happen during the game?"

"What do you mean by that?"

"I mean to ask if, let's say, somebody came in when you were playing or things that happened that shouldn't have happened?"

"Emily came in with the coffee. Other than that, I think—wait! Alvin came home before the coffee was served, but I really don't know what time that was. I can't give an estimate either. I'm sorry."

"That's all right. You're quite sure nothing else of interest happened?"

"Yes, I am. But give me a moment anyway. I want to make sure I tell you everything now, so we don't have to do this anymore. Just let me think."

We did, and after what seemed like years, she ejaculated an excited 'Ah!'.

"I remember something else now! Just before the coffee was served, about five minutes I think, I saw Bobby and Axel pace across the hallway; they were in a huge hurry. I only saw this out of the corner of my eye, but I think Axel peeped in quickly, then turned away. Maybe Bobby did too, but I can't be sure."

"That is of huge importance, Mrs. Farell! Thank you for remembering it. What about Geraldine's will? Did she have one? Do you know what is in it?"

"She had a will; that much I do know. But even I, her own sister, don't know what's in it! Can you believe that? So, I'm sorry but I can't help you out with that. You have to ask our lawyer or Agnes because she's arranging the date for the will to be read out. Is that all?"

"There is just one more thing: you *are* sure it was Alvin who came in through the front door?"

My heart started beating furiously fast now. This was important! This was what I hoped to experience when I came here with Andrew!

"Yes, I should think. I heard the door open and close and it *must* simply be him! Who else left the house that night?"

"But you didn't *actually* see him?"

"No, I didn't," she said slowly. "But I'm quite sure that it was him all the same. If there's nothing left, may I leave now?"

"Yes, yes, you may. Thank you very much; you have been most informative."

When she had left, I insisted Andrew tell me what was on his mind. Many things perhaps, but I didn't care. I had waited too long.

"That woman is very observant, and if she's told us nothing but the absolute truth, then we have just taken one very large step closer to ending this game. Yes, definitely, I wish we approached her first. Even then, there is something she said that doesn't quite fit into my idea of what's going on. Something, but I'm not sure what yet. But I can, indeed sense victory to be one step closer!"

Bobby

We left the study room and asked Sebastian if there was anybody home whom we could talk to. He put his finger to his chin in an 'I'm-wise-and know-more-than-you' manner which, I admit, was highly annoying. "Even if you didn't respect me, at least respect Andrew Sommers!" But what I really said was "Well?"

And at last, he said, "I think Bobby and his friend are upstairs. Would you please follow me to their room?" So we did.

We walked up the flight of creaking wooden stairs, me keeping my hands steadily on the banister for I was paranoid and quite certain the stairs would give way underneath my feet.

Finally, we reached the top. I was breathless. I was panting. I was *fat*. But of course, Andrew and even old Sebastian walked swiftly as if they had not just gone through some vigorous training but instead, had just gotten up from a chair or something like that. But I didn't want to embarrass myself further, so I put all I had into keeping up with them.

I was, however, able to observe a little of the upstairs of the mansion; partly due to the fact that there really was little to observe. Once at the top, one could either turn to the left or right, along a single, straight hallway. Unlike the downstairs that indeed resembled a labyrinth, the layout of this floor was fairly simple; all was plain to the eye. We turned left.

The walls were covered with sand-brown wall paper, plain without any motif or theme. The first door on our right was rather small and not as majestic-looking as the rest I must say. But no further speculation was necessary because Sebastian said, "Toilet," and mumbled "if you need it."

Then, on our left was a very large space, the lounge presumably, complete with a comfy sofa set and a television. Upon closer inspection, I noticed that there was a very sophisticated sound-surround system installed, a glass table (matched everything nicely, as glass always does) with nothing on it and, further back, a drinks bar! Now, this was an exciting place to spend time in! There were several glasses and plates and a few jars of cookies and biscuits on the counter. But, no bottled drinks, just a water kettle and glass jug, half-full with water.

While I was busy daydreaming about what I would do if I had such a lounge, Sebastian was knocking on the door directly opposite.

"Bobby? Axel?"

The door was literally flung open very suddenly and a teenage boy with thick, black hair that covered most of his ears glared at Sebastian.

"What do you want? I thought I told—" He stopped abruptly when he caught sight of us. "Who are you?" he asked in the same haughty manner.

"Andrew Sommers at your service," Andrew said gallantly.

"And I'm Tony Philipps," I said, scratching out my part as Andrew's assistant.

He looked dumbstruck for a while, then his attitude took a hundred eighty degrees turn and he was polite, humble and everything else that didn't appear possible a mere few seconds ago. I almost laughed, but pinched myself on the leg just in time.

"Ax-Axel! It's them! Remember the ones Aunt Agnes told us would be coming?"

At this point of time, Sebastian took his leave, saying," You can take care of things from here, I'm sure." Andrew nodded and thanked him.

Axel appeared at the doorway. He was small-sized, shorter than Bobby and had a small head. His hair was tidier than Bobby (shorter hair) and he wore spectacles, tipped a little on one side. My first impression was 'nerdy' but he was charming in his own way. He extended his hand and shook Andrew's, then mine, smiling very . . . . well, it was the kind of smile that had nothing held back, the kind that made you feel comfortable and at ease immediately. Physically speaking, his appearance didn't change the scene much, but his personality was exploding; he was so lively and his optimism impacted us all. He seemed to move us with every word he uttered and the house no longer looked so gloomy. Though to be fair to everyone else, it wasn't his relative who died.

"Hi, I'm Axel. Nice to meet you."

"Yes, I'm Andrew and he's Tony. The pleasure is ours."

There was a brief moment of awkward silence after the simple exchange of pleasantries, shattered at last when Andrew turned to Axel and said, "Could we have some time with Bobby alone?"

"Yes, of course," Axel said. "I'll wait downstairs."

Bobby stepped aside and let us into his room, shutting the door after himself. I have to say that the room was very typical of a teenager's room. In the corner closest to the cupboard was Bobby's computer table. The computer had been left on and the screensaver was playing. Pipes. Standard. The walls were almost fully plastered with items like posters, drawings, a guitar, stick-it-notes, and the rest I shall refrain from recording here. The bed was a queen-sized bed, so I'm guessing before Axel was here, the fat slob had so much space to himself. Ok, I admit I don't like Bobby very much. His initial reaction to Sebastian revealed more about who he truly was compared to the saccharin-sweet smiles he was now flashing at us. To me, he was just a spoilt, rich kid who had no respect for anybody else, especially those poorer folks. The room was, however, tidier and neater than the norm.

Bobby pulled the chair from the computer table and placed it facing the bed. Then, grabbed his study table chair, knocked his school satchel off it thoughtlessly, and arranged the chair beside the first one.

"Sit," he said pointing to the chairs with his right index finger. His tone wasn't exactly rude, but rather that was what he was used to when talking to others. But I hated it then; still hate it now.

He himself crawled onto the comfort of his bed. We did as we were told and initiated the already familiar process.

"Bobby, which school do you attend?" A good ice-breaking question.

"I attend classes at Ballymore International School, the only international school in this town." I detected a tinge of arrogance in his voice, but no more.

"Can you tell me more about Axel?"

"You see Ballymore has sister schools located in a few other countries. They go by different names, but are all under the same umbrella. Axel is from Westwind Terrace International, Hong Kong. Our schools share a similar student exchange program and around this time of the year, every year, students from their school come and stay with students who are part of the program here. And in March, the reverse happens: we go to Hong Kong. I joined this program only in the middle of last year, and so I had missed the trip to Kong Kong. But I could still host a student in October and that student was Axel. We became very close friends after that and still keep in touch through Facebook. Axel likes many things that I like too. For example, we both like computer games and online games like Counter Strike and March of Madness. In fact, we were just playing that game when you came to this room. Perhaps you've heard of these games before?"

I shook my head but Andrew nodded his. Liar!

"When Axel is here, both of you attend lessons together at Ballymore. That's how student exchange programs work, right?"

"Yes, but our school has the week off starting Monday. So, I guess we'll be crazy with computer games, huh?"

Andrew smiled. "Can you tell me what you were doing and where you were after dinner the night your grand-aunt was poisoned?"

"After dinner, I think Axel and I came straight up to this room and started our online gaming session. It was around eight thirty, and I know we should have been studying or revising, but we had a really heavy meal and . . . ." He looked sheepishly at us before continuing, ". . . . well, my excuse is that I couldn't concentrate on Maths or English grammar on a full stomach. And it was a Friday night after all. So you see, I really wasn't in any *mood* for studying."

"Please do get on with it; nobody cares about you studying or not that night!" But what I really said was: "Perfectly understandable", finishing off with "for a lazy bum like you" in my mind.

"Anyway, we were playing War of Chaos, and that game requires, um, focus, and we had on our headphones, so we couldn't and didn't hear anything that happened outside our room. I can't be of much help to you in that sense, you understand?"

"Yes, and what time did you sleep?"

"The minutes turned into hours, and before we knew it, the clock had already struck one, so to speak. We settled down and fell asleep by half past one I think."

"You don't know what time your grandmother and grand aunt went to bed then?"

"Oh, yes, um, I think it was half past midnight. The hallway lights are left on until everybody goes to bed. The last one to bed switches the lights off and so on. There's a mirror on the wall right above my computer, right there, see?" He pointed at the mirror which was behind us.

"Yes, so?" I asked.

"That night, our room was particularly stuffy and I felt it was no good to be cooped up like that. Axel suggested we open the window but it was simply too windy that night and all my work assignments were scattered everywhere. So, we left the door slightly, very slightly, ajar instead. Now, from where I was sitting, I saw Geraldine come up at the top of the stairs, then, on instinct, I checked my watch. And yes, now I'm sure it was exactly at 12:37 a.m. when she came up." He finished triumphantly. "She turned off the lights, since she thought she was the last to bed. Of course, she didn't know we were still awake then."

"Wait, do you mean to say that you can and did indeed see everybody coming up the stairs?"

"Yes, but only at the top; so I can't see what's going on, let's say, a bit further down. Why don't you have a look for yourself?"

Bobby left the door slightly ajar, being careful to leave it as it was that Friday night. We looked into the mirror and saw the head of the stairs just as he described. The gap was just wide enough to make out who was at the top, assuming there was somebody there. Satisfied, we all resumed our seats.

"Does anybody else know you saw who came up and went down that night other than us?"

"Well, I didn't tell anybody, but, maybe, Axel knows because he knows we left the door open, though he might not know that I could see clearly enough through the gap."

"Alright, don't tell anybody; I think it's best that way. So, who *did* you see going up and down the stairs that night?"

"Wow, that's a hard one. I'll have to think for a moment."

There was a pause before he continued, "After dinner, Axel, both my parents, Aunt Agnes and I all came up together. Uncle Alvin went out. I'm not sure for what though. Then, I remember seeing Agnes go downstairs while waiting for my computer to boot up. So, that's around eight thirty I think; or slightly before that. She went down to bake, that much I know. And not long after we began playing, I saw Alvin come upstairs. Wait again, please. The times are all messed up inside my head." Another pause. "I think that was eight forty-five, or was it eight forty? I suppose five minutes doesn't matter too much, right?"

"Did anybody else go down besides Agnes?"

"Wait! I forgot to tell you this! It's really important! Err . . ." Suddenly he was at a loss of words.

"What is it?" I asked.

"Axel and I went down. We were looking for Axel's game sheet for the game. There are tips and input methods for different commands on it. I was reluctant at first, but Axel insisted I help him. He said we'd be faster if we searched together, so I agreed. We went to the kitchen first to ask Emily if she had seen it, but she said 'no'. Axel told her it was really important to him and of course, she put the pot she was holding down and came out to help us look. Agnes was there too, baking as I said, but her hands were already clean because the cookies were in the oven by then, so she offered to help as well. She said she'd seen a piece of paper with strange symbols on it lying around somewhere, but she said she'd forgotten where. The four of us combed the entire downstairs, all the while being careful not to disturb the mahjong game, but inevitably, we had to pass the room they were in to search the living room. I'm not sure if they saw us though. Finally, Agnes found it under some books in the study. Relief. After that, they went back to whatever they were doing in the kitchen, and we came back here." He was almost completely out of breath by this time. His beetroot-red face was comical to observe. I really am a terrible person, am I not?

"That is indeed very exciting! But what happened next?"

"Well, slightly past nine, Agnes came up and came towards us to use the washroom, the one beside this room. I think that nobody used this staircase till my granny and her sister."

"Did they come up together or separately?"

"My granny came up a few minutes before Geraldine. They stay in separate rooms, you know."

"Was there anything different about Geraldine when she came up?"

"I didn't really observe her, but I should think not."

"Ok, tell me, Bobby, what do you think of your Aunt Agnes and Uncle Alvin? And also, your late grand aunt?"

"I like Aunt Agnes. She's—you won't tell anybody about what I say now, will you? I prefer these opinions of mine kept strictly between us."

Andrew nodded, smiling at him. Was it just me? Or did that same smile of his bring about a different meaning depending on the circumstance? It felt like Mona Lisa; but in reference to his smile, not the 'eyes' part. "Of course," Andrew said.

"As I was saying, Aunt Agnes is the kind of aunt anybody would like to have. She's unmarried, and she likes children," he said, waving his hand suggestively at himself. "She is kind and young at heart, not like my mother who seems so old compared to her. Aunt Agnes also plays board games with me sometimes, not computer games though (regretfully), and she drives me around when I have activities, you know, like meeting up with friends and so on. And she's so proud of me as her nephew. I know she talks a lot about me to those rich socialite friends of hers. And lastly, surely you must have noticed by now, Aunt Agnes is a very, very classy person! I like that part about her most! Somehow, she really stands out in a crowd."

Undeniable, I thought to myself.

"That was a very kind thing to say about your aunt. Yes, she sounds like a great aunt to have indeed! What about your uncle?"

"I'm sorry to say I don't like him as much as I like Aunt Agnes. But obviously, it's not very fair for me to say that because I've only known him for a month, and furthermore, he keeps to himself a lot. I rarely see him in the house, let alone chatting with, well, the rest of us," he said, making another gesture with his hand. "When we do meet, he rarely smiles at me. It's normally just me greeting him and on those rare occasions when he feels high or something like that, he bothers to acknowledge me." He finished sarcastically.

"Wow, he's a pretty hard person to get along with then. How does the rest of your family cope with his behaviour?" Andrew asked.

"I think he treats the adults better. In fact, I'm sure he does. It's just Axel and me who suffer the most around him. Axel was like me in the beginning; he smiled and greeted him too, but after a while of receiving nothing but the cold shoulder from him, he gave up. Now, according to Axel, when they walk past each other along the hallways, they treat it as if the other didn't exist!" He laughed a little. "But for Axel, it's fine because in a short while's time, he will be going home; but this is home for me. Looks like I'm stuck here with him."

"And Mrs. Geraldine?" What is she like?"

"She . . . . she could have been nicer," Bobby managed after some hesitation. "I mean she wasn't a bad person, she was just—it's hard to say what she's like really. I would say stingy, yet loving. She doesn't really show her love in very vivid forms, but it just emanates from her. If you had lived with her, even just for a week, you'd understand what I mean. But when I say 'stingy', I really mean it. She wouldn't even part with a few pennies to buy me sweets; oh, I've asked before, when I was younger, of course. I know what I'm saying seems to be contradictory, but it's the truth. I suppose one could be both loving and stingy at the same time."

"Yes, that is indeed possible," said Andrew.

There was a brief moment of silence in the room as Andrew was deep in thought. Finally, he said, "Yes, I think we're done here. Could you please go downstairs and tell Axel to meet us here? And when we're ready, we'll go down and you can come back into the room. Thank you."

It was an awkwardly constructed sentence, and rather crude, but I suppose Andrew wanted to make sure that Bobby wouldn't come back in to interrupt our discussion with Axel. Bobby merely nodded and left the room. The door closed with a soft thud behind him.

Axel

"So far, all the versions tally, which means nobody is lying . . . . yet," I said doubtfully.

"Not necessarily correct, Philipps. You see, they could have planned all this out and rehearsed it a million times if they needed to cover something as a, um, team."

"So, you think one of them is lying, or they're all lying?"

"Still, it's too early. There are many more people we need to question before we can safely conclude anything."

We heard a sharp knock on the door just then and Axel opened the door without waiting for an answer and came in, closing the door behind him.

"Hello, Axel!" said Andrew.

"Hello, detectives," Axel said, smiling at us once more, then glanced at the bed. The mess (pillows in disarray and blanket unfolded and strewn all over the bed) that Bobby left behind indicated where Axel was to sit.

It was a few seconds before Axel turned towards us apologetically and said, "I'm sorry. I don't feel comfortable discussing this issue here. Can we please perhaps go somewhere else?"

"Yes, it's up to you. It was getting a bit stuffy here anyway," Andrew said.

Axel merely nodded in relief and opened the door once more. He left it open for us this time. I went out, closely followed by Andrew, who pulled the door behind him.

"So, it's the study then?" Axel asked, heading towards the stairs.

"Yes, that's a good place."

We followed him down, but at the middle of the stairs, Andrew exclaimed "Wait a minute!" Then, he groped around in his shirt pocket and said, "I think I left my pen in your room. It must have fallen off me onto the bed when I got up. Please excuse me; I'll see you in the study."

"No problem," Axel said and continued down the stairs. I flashed Andrew a suspicious look, then quickly followed Axel, who was almost at the bottom of the stairs. Andrew was up to something! I could sense it!

We passed Bobby in the living room. He looked at us, but said nothing, and we said nothing to him. Eventually, we ended up in the study, where I resumed my seat. Yes, pretty much it was *my* seat now. We were joined almost immediately by Andrew, who had a pen in his pocket. I had never seen it before, but that could be due to my lack of observance.

"Found it!" he said triumphantly.

"Good for you," said Axel.

When we were all seated, Andrew began asking his questions.

"Axel, tell us about yourself."

"I'm from Hong Kong. I study at Westwind Terrace International School, and I think you already know I'm here on a student exchange program. We—I mean Bobby and I—are the same age; we're both fifteen. And, I think Bobby would already have told you this, but, we're both computer game fanatics. That night when *it* happened, we were engrossed with games, and to make matters worse, it was a Friday night and we were like 'There's no school tomorrow!' and all that, so I remember we were up till pretty late. Oh, sorry, I've strayed too far off topic!" He looked apologetic.

"It's ok. Can you give us a little background on your family?"

This question came as a shock to me, and apparently to Axel as well.

"I beg your pardon? My family?" His disbelief was vividly displayed on his face.

"Yes, I think it will help some way or another, but if you refuse to, I suppo—"

"No, it's alright, it's alright." Axel regained his composure, cutting Andrew off, but I suspect that Axel was playing into his hands already, though why Andrew wanted to know about his family, I don't know. "My family is quite well-off. My father is a civil engineer who has profit-sharing in huge housing projects all over Hong Kong. The price of property there has experienced a recent boom, and of course, my family benefits greatly from that. My mother is a full-time lecturer in the University of Hong Kong. I'm an only child, so whatever my parents own will someday be mine. There! Are you satisfied?" he said sarcastically, with a tinge of acid satisfaction at the end.

"Do your parents know about anything that's been happening here?"

"No; I simply told them the time frame for the exchange program had been extended. Indefinitely. They don't mind; they're too busy with work to care anyway."

"You were here last year around this time, weren't you?"

"Yes."

"I need you to think very carefully now. Is there anything, no matter how seemingly unimportant, different about this house and/or the people in it now compared to during your last visit?"

"Well, that's easy. Alvin showed up." Axel's voice was spiteful, yet controlled.

"Alvin?"

"Yes, Bobby's uncle. Have you met him?"

"I must say not yet."

"Good for you once more," Axel half-whispered, then quickly saying, "Oh, do forgive me for being this immature; I must tell you that I don't particularly like him, but let's not allow him to distract us from the issue at hand. Where were we?"

"Any changes here since last year?"

"Oh, yes! *That!* Let me think," he said, and a considerable pause entered the conversation. Finally, he said, "I don't think so. I mean Bobby's still, well . . . . Bobby! And Miss Agnes and Bobby's parents are as kind as ever. And Granny Gina and Geraldine are still the typical old people. Gina seems to be keeping everything under control at home as usual and Emily treats me well even though she's under little obligation to. And you already know how I feel about Alvin, so there you have it."

"You missed out Geraldine."

"No, I didn't. I mentioned her—"

"You mentioned she was a typical old woman, but what exactly do you mean by that?"

"I'm sorry, Mr. Sommers, but that's as far as I go as far as she's concerned. My parents have always taught me to respect the dead, so me bad-mouthing her now would be completely inappropriate. I'm sorry."

Hah! Despite my flaws, I was sharp enough to realize that Axel had let his tongue slip, purposely or otherwise I know not, but he had just revealed that he disliked Geraldine. 'Bad-mouthed' was the word he used. He would only use it if he had complains about her!

"That's understandable. Then, we should move on. Can you give us your version of what happened that night, starting from after dinner?"

"I was expecting you to ask that. After dinner, Mrs. Geraldine, Gina, Emily and Debbrah played mahjong in the dining room. Everybody, as far as I know went upstairs, but I can't be sure because Bobby and I were the first ones up. We were rushing you see, for two reasons. The first was because we had been planning to hit the computers; I'm sure Bobby already told you we were gaming till early morning, right?

"Yes, he did."

"The second is that, don't laugh please, we wanted to 'escape' from the older folks for fear that they might need extra players for their game or if they had any funny ideas about making us run errands for them or things like that. And we don't like to disrespect them, so the best way was just to be obscurely hidden away in our rooms. But I heard after the whole incident that Miss Agnes was in the kitchen that night with Emily, and Alvin left the house for a while. So, it's obvious that my first impression was wrong and that *not* everybody was up like I've mentioned earlier." He took a pause.

"Anyway, we started playing, and I don't really remember anything else that happened till about one when we decided to call it a night, or morning. Whatever."

"Just to get a clearer picture of the whole scenario, where were you seated while playing? Bobby was at his computer table, but where was your laptop or notebook?"

"I was on the bed, facing the window, but why—I mean, how will that help in any way?"

"Now isn't the time for such questions to be answered; it is merely the time to collect all the pieces of the puzzle. The piecing part always comes later. Also,

Axel, you wouldn't know who came up the stairs and when, would you?"

"No, I didn't notice anything after I started playing. I know, nerdy, right?"

"So, you're saying that you did absolutely nothing but play that night till the time you fell asleep?"

"Yes."

"All right, Bobby told us about the game sheet issue. Perhaps you would like to elaborate?" There was a hint of poison in Andrew's voice. The first time I've heard it.

At this point of time, Axel's face underwent a sudden metamorphosis. His smile vanished into thin air, and it was as if a sudden shadow was cast over all of us.

Very, very reluctantly, he said, "Well, to be completely honest with you, I was hoping you'd never find out that we went downstairs for that game sheet. But, I guess I'm being naïve because you were bound to find out sooner or later. And that Bobby is foolish. He doesn't even realize that going down at that unfortunate time has made us suspects, if not even prime suspects! And looking back, if I had known she was going to die, I would never for my life have gone downstairs to be involved in all that. I mean, if we were in our room, we were safe, and I know you look at me, at us, in a different light now, don't you? As if we were the murderers!"

"Nobody's accusing anybody yet. It's just—"

"Forget it. After all, if I truly were the murderer, you'd find out anyway. So, I guess, conversely, if I am really innocent, even if there was proof of me placing my *whole hand* into the cup, I'd be safe. So, yes, we did go downstairs for my game sheet. We went into the kitchen to enlist Emily's help. Agnes was there too. Together, we searched the whole of downstairs, and finally, Agnes found it in the library. And, yes, if you must know, we did pass the old women playing mahjong, but we were in a rush, so we didn't care about them, and I suppose they ignored us too. I can tell you also, for a fact, that I didn't enter the kitchen again that night. We went straight up. And this time, I'm not keeping anything from you anymore. Happy?"

His tone was full of spite and he no longer offered any smiles, only sneers.

"A word of caution to the wise: don't try to keep anything from me. You'd be surprised at how much I know!" Andrew ended with a jolly tone. I was surprised. Still am to this day how he managed that. The tension was stressful on all of us.

"Yes, no doubt, I'd be surprised." This time, Axel had regained some, if not most, of his composure. If he ever harboured any feelings of dislike toward Andrew he certainly showed little of it now.

"I have more questions I'd like to ask, but perhaps now isn't the best time."

"Yes, you're right once more. Have a good day, Mr. Sommers, Mr. Philipps."

He left the room. The tension was released instantaneously. I could feel my breathing return to normal, and my palms stopped sweating. That went terribly, though I never mentioned that to Andrew.

I looked at Andrew inquisitively. Did he just make a mistake; do something he never planned to? Did he finally lose his eloquence, and in so doing, offended or threatened one of the key suspects? Or could Axel himself be guilty or knew who the guilty one was? And did Andrew, at this point of time, already know the answers to those questions?

"Well, is he—is he guilty?"

"I don't know yet."

That was the first time I heard him admit his lack of knowledge. Normally, he'd sidestep the issue with some cunningly crafted response, the kind I had grown so accustomed to. Andrew had a distant look in his eyes; he was obviously in thought once more. But *I* wasn't. And I wasn't prepared to let him bore me to death with his silence.

"He seemed pretty guilty to me towards the end there. What was he thinking? That he could actually conceal something as huge as that from us?"

"His concern that we might immediately place him on the list of prime suspects if we ever found out he went downstairs is fully justified. And we did, didn't we?

I nodded.

"It's just as he said: he was perfectly safe had he stayed in the room upstairs or if we never found out. Also, he was right to say it was an 'unfortunate' time to be downstairs. Coincidence? Maybe. Maybe not. But what surprises me more is the depth to which Axel understood the implications of his and Bobby's seemingly simple act of going downstairs for the game sheet. Incidentally, Bobby, until now, doesn't even realize the danger he had put himself in, and also Axel, by revealing such information. Of course, of course, we would have found out anyway, but do you remember how *excited* he was to tell us? I can't help but laugh at his naivety now as I look back. And finally, to complicate matters, now both Bobby and Axel are suspects. Either that, or one, or maybe even both of them, *knows* who did it. They might just not realize they know until it's too late. That means they're not safe!"

"I wouldn't worry about Bobby if I were you. He wouldn't know who the murderer was even if he or she *told* him! It's Axel. He's in some serious trouble if he does know who did it."

"Let's pray they stay safe. Anyway, would you like to know what I discovered when I went back up alone earlier? You remember, don't you, for my pen?"

"Oh, yes! I meant to ask. You deliberately left it in his room, didn't you?"

"I could have done that. Or . . . . I could have left it in my pants pocket the whole time and only taken it out on the pretext that I had 'found' it in the place I never left it to begin with! Yes, the latter is easier and less problematic. Anyway, I didn't re-enter the bedroom, believe it or not!"

"Then, what was all the drama for?" I was a tinge disappointed, expecting him to have found some form of evidence that was to set this mystery straight immediately.

"I was only interested in the *door*."

"The door?"

"Yes. Or rather what one could see beyond it!"

"Beyond the door? That means the room. Have you gone mad?"

"Oh, no! Not the room, the mirror and what it reflected! Do you understand my little experiment now?"

"No," I said flatly.

Andrew sighed before continuing.

"Philipps, remember what Bobby said earlier? He said he could see everybody at the top of the stairs through that mirror, so long as the door was left open, or in our case, slightly ajar. Now the only question remaining in that whole concept is whether anybody could see Bobby through that same gap!"

"So, could they?"

"That was part of my experiment! I left the door ajar the same way Bobby had demonstrated to us and looked in from the outside, first from the stairs, then a little closer, from the lounge. And guess what? In both cases, the door appeared *shut*! It's some sort of illusion that tricks the brain, caused by the toning and colour of the walls and arrangement of furniture in the room! In fact, one can only see the door is ajar a few feet away from the room, and only upon *very* careful scrutiny. That means Bobby could have seen the murderer descend and/or ascend without giving himself away! That's of extreme significance!"

"Yes, yes, that's all very good but do you trust Bobby to provide accurate information? And that's assuming he *has* such information to begin with! He could have missed the murderer while focusing on his desktop screen, for example."

"Sadly, you're right, and that only complicates things. But try, Philipps."

"Try what?"

"Try being nice to Bobby. Admit it! You don't like him!"

"You mean that fat slob? Oops, you mean that, erm (I paused to try to think of anything good about Bobby), *authoritative* boy?"

"Good improvement, but I'd give you an 'F' for results."

"All right, all right, what's next?"

"Let's try . . . . Dr. Marion. But not today for sure. We have made good progress thus far, and we're both tired."

Dr. Marion

We went back out into the hallway and caught sight of Sebastian, his hand on the door knob, coat and hat on, obviously about to retire for home. I checked my watch. It was only five forty-nine. Agnes said it was six when he was supposed to go home I remember.

"Sebastian?" Andrew called out. No answer. It was impossible for him not to have heard.

"Sebastian?" he repeated. The door was virtually flung open inwards as he shifted his body out of the house.

"Sebastian, is this handkerchief yours? Right over here?" he tried, just as he quickly dropped his own onto the carpet.

The door was closed as rapidly as it was opened and Sebastian turned around to face us, his expression catatonic.

"Is that so?" he asked, gliding over to us.

Upon closer inspection, he said it wasn't his, but he would leave it on the table and ask the others tomorrow.

"Yes, that's a good idea. Is Miss Agnes home by the way?"

"Yes, she came home when you were in Bobby's room. She knows you're here; I told her, and she said she wouldn't interrupt then."

"Can I speak to her now?"

"I should think so. At the top of the stairs, turn right, it's the second room on the left, beside the toilet."

"The same bathroom as before? Sorry, I'm a little confused."

"No, there are two bathrooms upstairs that are not attached to any room. The one you saw earlier is smaller."

"Yes, thank you."

We plodded—or rather *I* plodded (Andrew just walked)—up the stairs again, and as we did, I could practically read Sebastian's thoughts: "Finally, they're gone! Best leave before they ask me to do anything else for them!"

At the top, we turned right, and found the room just as he had told us, and knocked. Agnes came out, wearing a simple pink blouse with no makeup on or hair done. First time we'd seen her like that I realized.

"Good evening, Agnes. I just wanted you to know that we're leaving now. We'll come back tomorrow."

"How are things so far?" Who have you spoken to?"

"I must say I'm surprised. Today has been an exceptionally productive day. So far, we've already spoken to Emily, your mother, Bobby and Axel, and, of course, you."

"I suppose it's a little too soon, but do you have any answers yet?"

"No, it's as you say; a little too soon, regretfully."

"Um, I hate to say this, but I guess I have to, for the good of the family." She paused. "If, and I mean if, and I don't mean to insult you or anything like that, but if after doing all you can and you fail to come up with anything solid, please, please, don't, oh, how do I say this, please don't, um, simply fire accusations at any one of us. Things are very delicately balanced around here, and I guess the truth is none of us really want to hear that this is a murder case, let alone know who the murderer is. I know what I'm saying is morally wrong, and the truth should always prevail and all that, but try. Try to understand us. We are all wishing it was a suicide and nothing more, as unlikely as that may be. And of course, we'll still pay you accordingly regardless of the results of your investigation, whether you fail or succeed. And we'll do our best to keep this between us, so as not to ruin your career. I'm so very sorry to have said all that, to doubt you, but I think, yes, I think that an answer is not likely. Even if you are one of the most famous detectives of our generation. You see, the police have already asked everything there is to be asked, and searched everywhere there is to be searched. I doubt there is much more you can do."

She finally stopped, her face blushing red with embarrassment. An awkward moment for all of us I must say. How would Andrew respond? I was slightly worried.

"Yes, yes, I suppose if I were you I'd feel this way as well. But rest assured, I *will* get to the bottom of this. If I don't, I will, of course, not accept any payment and I won't attempt any more cases henceforth. What I do regret is *when* I get to the bottom of this, and it is indeed a murder case, I cannot lie to any of you and tell you it was a suicide. Do you understand? I simply must expose the guilty one; that's the way it should be. However, I will not interfere with what you *choose* do with the truth. That's my stand. It always has been."

"That's acceptable, but only when you're sure that's the truth, and nothing else."

"Yes."

"Right, would you like to stay for dinner? It'll be at half past seven as usual, about an hour from now. You'll be able to meet everybody at last, because all of us stay in for dinner."

"That's a kind offer, but I'm afraid we're rushing to the bus station to catch the 6:45 home."

"Oh, I see. Well, some other time then."

"Before I go, can you give me Dr. Marion's house phone number? I only have his clinic's number. You see, tomorrow's Sunday, and we hope to catch him on a day when he has no appointments, and preferably we'd like to meet him in his house, not in his clinic."

"Yes, I think he wouldn't mind. He's a nice man, you know. Here."

She took out her cell phone from her pocket and read his number out. Andrew saved it on his cell phone, and for a second there, I was tempted to produce my phone as well, just to match the technological festival that was suddenly taking place.

"I've also already told him about you helping out with this case but please call before you drop by at his house, and mention my name. He might have forgotten about the whole issue by now. You know how it is with doctors, always so busy!"

"Yes, of course. Goodbye. I will come by tomorrow after lunch, or maybe around tea time depending on how long we take with Dr. Marion. Do you have any plans then?"

"I think Bobby and Axel might be at the sports club again, but the rest of us should be in. Do drop by. Goodbye."

We left the mansion for home. The journey home was uneventful, but we did have a big dinner (detective work makes me hungry) before we parted ways. Andrew told me he planned to call Dr. Marion that night and that I should meet him tomorrow at his house around nine.

Day one of this case was officially over. I felt a strange sense of fulfilment, though I had no good reason to.

* * *

The next morning, sharp at nine, I knocked on Andrew's door. His butler let me in with a warm smile on his wrinkled face.

"Good morning, Mr. Philipps. Come in, come in," he said, immediately stepping aside and taking my coat and hat off me.

I'd rank him infinite times higher than Sebastian from Stevenson Mansion, just between us.

"Mr. Sommers is in his study. You know the way, don't you?"

"Yes, yes, see you later."

But at that point of time, Andrew himself took the liberty of saving me the trouble of further walking by emerging from the hallway entrance.

"Punctuality. Good. Let's go then."

"Yes, good morning to you too," I chuckled.

We went to Little Flattington in Andrew's car this time. Along the way the conversation ran along the lines of:

"So, you've informed Dr. Marion that we'll be visiting him today?"

"Yes, he's expecting us. Don't worry, I called him last night and everything's already been arranged."

"And what's his address?"

"16, Greenwood Avenue, near the town's main park."

"It shouldn't be too hard to find then."

But I was dead wrong. We reached Little Flattington at around nine twenty. And we only found his house close to ten. The search made me almost dizzy, what with all those junctions and similar road names, but we made it. A gentleman in his late forties, in casual wear answered the door.

"Mr. Sommers and friend, right?" he asked.

"Yes, good morning. And you are Dr. Marion?"

"Yes, come in, I've been expecting you."

He seemed like a nice man. Quite humble. Led a simple life. His house was small compared to the Farells' or to Andrew's for that matter, but not any less of a home. No butler. Simple furnishing. But for once, we needed this sort of environment for the investigation. Running around in large mansions all day long, looking for so-and-so was *not* the way to go.

We hung our coats and hats and followed him into the living room. When we were seated, Dr. Marion asked if we would like anything to drink. I was on the verge of saying 'yes', but Andrew's 'no, thank you' discouraged me. Fine. No drinks then.

"Thank you for sparing us some time on a Sunday like this."

"Oh, no problem. There'll always be another Sunday for me to sleep in on," he joked.

"I trust you know the nature of our visit; I told you on the phone last night."

"Yes, about Geraldine's death. Please, just ask anything you want."

"First of all, how long have you been their family doctor?"

"Eighteen years. At that time, Geraldine was fifty-three. She found me after her ex-family doctor retired."

"Can you tell me about Geraldine's medical background?"

"I would say she is quite healthy for her age, and if she hadn't been poisoned, I think she would have had another ten years coming her way. She had a few problems; for instance, she developed minor heart attacks a couple of years ago, but she always had the appropriate medication with her and those problems never got serious. Besides, there is another doctor in the family now, isn't there? James, I think. So, she was fine as far as her health was concerned. She also complained about muscle aches every now and then. I told her it was normal for any aging person, but she could relieve the pain by regular exercise. She told me she intended to do brisk walking every morning, but I don't know how far that is true. That's about it I think. Of course, there were also the occasional bouts of flu, but that happens to everybody."

"I see. Nothing more serious than that?"

"Afraid not."

"Did you do the autopsy?"

"No, they felt it was better to send her to the hospital, um, Bellefort Hospital; it's here in Little Flattington actually. They had showed me the autopsy report, so I can answer questions regarding that for you.

By the way, have you spoken to James yet? He works there."

"No, actually. So, what was the poison that did it?" Andrew wanted to be sure.

"Strychnine. That's what the report said. It tallies with the report from the police department as to what was in the cup of coffee that night. So, she *did* get poisoned during the mahjong game. Quite interesting, if not very fortunate, I must say."

"Can you give us a little background on that poison? I'm sorry I don't know very much about poisons."

"Strychnine comes in the form of odourless, bitter, transparent crystals. They are insoluble in normal water, but slightly soluble in boiling water, and even more soluble in alcohol. I suppose Geraldine didn't know what the small crystals in her coffee cup were; probably thought they were just sugar crystals that had not been dissolved yet. After all, coffee is bitter, so she wouldn't have been able to taste the difference."

"What does strychnine do to your body?"

"It causes muscle contractions and convulsions, therefore the victim may experience muscle aches and spasms and also stiffness in certain parts. A small dose is fatal. It kills by eventually exhausting the respiratory muscles, so you wouldn't be able to breathe and die from lack of oxygen. I supposed she died in her sleep and couldn't get any help in time. If it *wasn't* a suicide that is to say."

"How long does it take for the symptoms to be seen after ingestion?"

"Within half an hour to an hour."

"Oh, but did you know she ingested the poison at nine, and went to bed at half past midnight? Wouldn't the symptoms have been seen way before that? She should have been in time to get help from her sister or neighbours, right?"

"Yes, I find that rather strange, actually. The report estimated the time of death to be around one, which contradicts the effects of the poison. If I'm right, she should have shown the symptoms of poisoning by eleven latest. I've put a lot of thought into it. And I think I might know why nobody noticed until it was too late. I think that since the strychnine crystals were insoluble in the coffee, she only ingested very, very little of it, so little that she could breathe normally till, let's say, midnight. And maybe she did feel a little stiffness, but blamed it on the fact that she was glued to her chair with minimal movement for hours in a row. And her spasms? Maybe too small to notice. And besides, knowing her, she would have ignored them for the sake of the game. But I'm surprised she could make it up the stairs. I can't think of any way in which she could have managed that!"

There was a momentary silence as Andrew contemplated all the information that had just been provided. Finally, he said:

"But I suppose for now, we have to take it at face value for what it is. One never knows how exactly the body responds to poisons, and yes, her dosage might have been too mild for violently visible symptoms. And, for all we know, the poison could have been administered later in the game, but if that's the case, we can rule out many suspects."

My mind clicked into action now; if the poison really was administered later on during the course of the game, around eleven, maybe even later, then suspects like Agnes, Alvin, Bobby, Axel and Emily were ruled out! That leaves just Gina and the two neighbours.

"When was her last visit to you?" Andrew asked.

"Not in some time. March, I should say, when she complained about minor arm muscle aches, nothing serious really."

"In your opinion, did she kill herself? Or did someone really poison her?"

"Well, I suppose that's your job to find that out, isn't it? Not mine!"

"Yes, but you know her personality infinitely better than we do. So, you, for example, would know whether she was capable or likely to kill herself. Did she always think of the glass as half-full or half-empty? And so on."

"No, I don't think she would have done herself in."

"Why not?"

"Simply because she had a lot of 'fight' left in her. Whenever she came to me with a problem, she wouldn't take 'no' for an answer. And be it hard exercise or taking pills everyday, she could do it to stay alive. I guess she had suffered too much to just die without a fight. If you knew about her past, you'd understand what I mean. Yes . . . . I think she would even have murdered her murderer if she had known."

"Is she that vicious?"

"Well, I guess we'll never know."

"Thank you for your hospitality and time. I have no more questions for now. Have a nice Sunday, doctor."

"Yes, you too. Goodbye and all the best!"

And just like that, we left.

Alvin Farell

"We find ourselves at yet another unfortunate time, Philipps," said Andrew as we got into his car.

"How so?"

"It's noon now and if we drop by at the Farells', we wouldn't be able to conduct a full interrogation before lunch, which I assume to be at one."

"We could do it over lunch, couldn't we?"

"Yes, I suppose, but some people find it hard to concentrate on such heavy stuff over meals. You see, when people meet up for a meal, normally it's for light discussions or light conversations, not for such serious issues. But we'll see if the person in question is fine even over food."

"Who have you in mind?"

"I would like to meet Alvin or Bobby's parents; funny how we haven't seen them the whole of yesterday. Must be hiding from us!" laughed Andrew. "But it's really not in our control. We'll just have to see who's free to talk to us."

We arrived at Stevenson Mansion without much trouble, but it was a woman who answered the door, not Sebastian. A woman whom we've never met before. She was a blonde, with intricately formed features and a very exotic look. Really gorgeous; prettier than Agnes by far. I suspected that she was Audrey immediately; Gina wasn't kidding when she said she was attractive!

"Yes, how can I help you?"

"Good afternoon. I'm Andrew Sommers and this is Tony Philipps. We're the detec—"

"Oh! You're the detectives Agnes called to help us! How silly of me not to have realized!" She laughed melodiously, and suddenly, she became very conscious of her looks; her fingers hurried to tidy her hair and she arranged her white blouse (though that was absolutely unnecessary). "Come in, come in!" She stepped aside and let us in.

"You must be Miss Audrey."

"Or Mrs. Tholson. People call me that more often," she said, smiling, revealing two rows of very glamorous teeth. And then it struck me that we never knew Bobby's surname until now. Tholson. Interesting.

"Audrey! Are you ready to go out?" shouted a man suddenly from upstairs.

"Yes, dear! I've been waiting downstairs for you."

Then, a well-dressed man appeared at the foot of the stairs. Upon seeing us, he stopped dead in his tracks and his manner became rigid.

"Well, hello. I'm sorry, but who are—"

"It's alright dear. They're the detectives Agnes told us about. They're here to, err, to—" She turned towards us and continued, "You never did tell me how I could help you! Is there anyone in particular whom you'd like to meet or something like that?"

"Since you quite obviously have plans, could we speak with Alvin? Is he in?"

"Yes," said James, still as rigid as ever. "I'm James. Nice to meet you, detectives." We shook hands.

"I'll go tell Alvin you're looking for him then, while you guys have a chat," said Audrey, smiling again.

"Yes, thank you."

"Are you two going out for lunch? I'm so sorry for interrupting," said Andrew, attempting to start a conversation.

"Yes, we were, actually. We have a reservation at some restaurant in town."

"When do you think you'll be back?"

"Well, I don't know. We'll be back when we get back I suppose." Still cold. I wondered what it would take to reach him; he was so distant. Almost as if he weren't even there talking to us.

"I hate to ask this question, and I know it's none of my business, but are you celebrating a special occasion?"

"Can't we have a nice lunch on a Sunday when we feel like it? I certainly hope you don't think we're celebrating Miss Geraldine's death, if that's what you were going at. And to be honest, there's nothing to celebrate, but I guess, that very nothingness is reason to celebrate in itself. Sometimes, like now, no news is good news." He smiled for the first time. I was impressed. Andrew had done it again.

"Yes, I never thought of it that way." Andrew smiled back.

"I know Agnes represented the majority of us when she asked you here to help out, but I honestly don't want you here. Not because I'm guilty, not because I have anything to hide. But simply because the dust has settled, and nothing tragic has happened since she passed. And when you come here, you unsettle the dust! Whatever evil that did it had died, but now it may live again! Don't you see? You, here, might just give the murderer reason enough to strike again. And I think all of us, and I mean *all*, would rather let the murderer escape scot-free, and no more deaths occur, than to reveal his or her identity and put us all at stake in so doing. We were home safe and sound, but now I have a hunch that . . . . we're not anymore. I know it must be crazy to think that we could possibly bear staying in this house when one of us is a cold-blooded murderer, but my family is at stake here! We're planning to move off, but even if we did stay, I'd rather live without ever knowing who did it, then watch my wife or son die." His tone was serious and concerned, but certainly not malicious or threatening in any way.

"Rest assured, we'll solve this before the murderer can even *think* of covering his tracks. But we'll need you to cooperate. Without your help, or anybody's for that matter, *nobody* is safe."

Audrey came down at that moment, with another man, Alvin, behind her. One good look at Alvin was enough to understand why Axel disliked him so much. He had a rugged look, poorly shaven moustache and beard; his lips were curved into a natural sneer, and when he smiled, his lips only curved upwards momentarily before resuming their original position. He looked like the murderer immediately to me, but I clamped my mouth shut to avoid blurting out any prejudiced words and tried instead to act normally.

"Mr. Sommers, Mr. Philipps, this is my brother, Alvin," said Audrey.

We shook hands and exchanged pleasantries. Alvin didn't do too badly in that aspect I must say.

"We'll leave you three alone and see you a bit later then," said James. "Come on, Audrey. Let's go."

Audrey hurriedly said 'goodbye' and left.

When we were alone, Andrew asked "We'd like to hear what you have to say about what happened the night your aunt was poisoned. And we also have some questions we'll need you to answer. Is that fine with you?"

"Yes, of course. Do you want to discuss this here or somewhere else?" Alvin's tone was meek and completely not suggestive of his appearance. A diamond-in-the-rough kind of person maybe. Who knows?

"Since it's almost time for lunch anyway, would you like to have this session over the meal? We won't have to rush then."

"Yes, let's go to, um—do you have any food preferences?"

"No, anything is fine for us."

"Then, I think we can go to the Spring & Autumn Café. It's within walking distance; I don't own a car you see. It's a nice, small little café where I know we won't be disturbed." That last sentence scared the living daylights out of me; was he planning on 'settling' us there?

But Andrew merely said, "Sounds good. Shall we?" said Andrew, heading towards the door. I hope Andrew was sure about this, but being such an experienced detective, he must know *some* self-defence techniques!

The walk was a pleasant one, during which we engaged in small talk with Alvin. First, we talked about the weather, then the culture and the people there, etc. He seemed really friendly, though I still had my reservations. But if it was real, then this would be the first time I had to disagree with Axel. Then again, this could just be a façade because of who we were, or rather who Andrew was.

After many turns and confusing streets, we reached the café. It was definitely small, and so obscure that I wondered if there were any customers other than us for the week! And when we went inside, I discovered that I was right. The only living person inside was a haggard-looking, lifeless waiter in his thirties sitting down by the cashier, flipping through the pages of . . . . *yesterday's* newspaper. Yup. Nobody's going to disturb us here for sure.

The place was very eccentrically designed. I say this because there were skulls (original or not, I don't know) on the wall instead of preserved animal heads, and bones where the photo frames should have been. The interior designer must have been *sick*!

I turned to Andrew, but he was still in cheerful conversation with Alvin. We took our seats where I thought would be the safest corner, the one with the least number of bones on the wall.

When asked for our orders, I only asked for a diet coke. Andrew gave me a look of disbelief, and I mumbled, "Lost my appetite."

"So, Alvin, can you tell us about yourself?" Andrew asked when the waiter had disappeared behind the kitchen door, which coincidentally was located beside the toilet. What a truly disgusting place.

"I am an accountant. I've worked in London before. In fact, I was just working there until a month ago, when I resigned and came home. I think you already know that, yes?"

"Yes, but we're not very sure why."

"I was stressed out and decided I needed a break. Just some time to be myself, then to look for a job someplace else. And where could I go but home?"

"Which company did you work for?"

"I managed the accounts of a J.J. Fast Food outlet in London. The outlet is relatively small and business wasn't very good, you see."

"Then, how come you became so stressed out? Accounts for a small business should have been easy enough."

"That's exactly the problem! Business got so bad that the main branch decided to fire the accountant from the branch nearest to mine, and then put me in charge of both accounts! I did that for a week, then resigned."

"I see, can I have your account of what happened the night Miss Geraldine was poisoned?"

"I don't know anything! What I can tell you you would have heard a dozen times by now!"

"Please, just try."

"Well, if you insist. We had dinner at around seven thirty, and finished at eight twenty I think. I went out after dinner to buy some 'smokes' from the store nearby. I took my jacket and sauntered out, walked really slowly to and fro, and I reached home slightly before nine."

I thought to myself, "Funny how everybody just *had* to be downstairs at the time of murder . . . ."

The food arrived, and Alvin continued speaking when the waiter was safely far away from us.

"When I got home, I immediately went upstairs. I didn't stop by at the mahjong table or study room or anything like that, and I didn't see anybody else. I went to bed early that night. I just felt so lethargic, I don't know why. And the next morning, Emily found her dead. Everything else is a blur to me now: the police, the tears, the questions, everything!"

"It's quite alright. What do you think of your aunt as a person?"

"She's . . . she's just stingy. Since I was a little boy till the day I left for London, she was the same. Calculative, miserly, cunning woman! But everything else about her was ok. She placed too much importance on her money, and forgot that what mattered more were the people she had in her life. And I suppose, someone finally decided to prove that her dollar bills should have meant nothing to her compared to us. Maybe, just, maybe, if she gave a little more freely, she'd still be alive today . . . ."

"So you think she was murdered for her money?"

"What else is there?"

"Maybe it was just suicide?"

"Suicide?" he had a very sarcastic look on his face. "I may have been away from home for a long time, but I know her well enough to know that she'd never do herself in."

"That is interesting to know. I think I have just one question left; do you know what was in your aunt's will?"

"No, I don't. I think none of us do, but if somebody did know, it'd be my mum. You should ask her. Anyway, Agnes said we'd deal with the will after you settled this case."

"Yes, she told us that as well."

The rest of the meal was in compete silence, shattered only by occasional small talk. But I was busy trying to piece this puzzle together. Maybe, I could beat Andrew to it and be the hero for once! Haha, that was a joke . . . .

James & Audrey Tholson

"**C**ould you show me the way to a drugstore? I need to buy something," Andrew asked just as we left the café.

"Yes, um, it's this way if I'm not mistaken."

And then begun another journey of twists and turns and unfamiliar lanes till I was quite lost. Eventually, we found our way to the same store Alvin visited on the 8th. I supposed being here for only around a month, he would patronize only one store, the one nearest to the mansion. Plus, I hadn't seen any other such stores in the area we were in. Andrew went in and bought a pack of cigarettes. He *doesn't* even smoke! But maybe, he just wanted to stage some sort of re-enactment of what happened that day, and probably to make sure they sold cigarettes in the first place. I know for a fact that some, if not many, drugstores didn't sell cigarettes. I'm not even sure if it's against the law for a drugstore to sell cigarettes.

"I didn't know you smoked," said Alvin.

"Neither did I," I thought to myself.

"A little."

We followed him home, but this time the route was fairly straightforward, the way it *should* be. Honestly, I don't believe life was ever meant to be *that* complicated; I mean the way Alvin does it, a square would appear to be some twenty-four sided three-dimensional shape.

As expected, James and Audrey weren't back yet, but Agnes was around according to Alvin, so we sent for her.

When Alvin was out of sight, Andrew told me, "You know I don't smoke; I just wanted to be sure he wasn't lying about that night."

"He still could be."

"But I believe him, don't you?"

"Yes, I do, and he's nothing like what Axel described him to be."

"That's still unclear, but—"

Agnes came down then and greeted us.

"What can I help you with?"

"I just want to ask you something about that night. Before you left the kitchen, before Emily served the coffee, something important happened. Am I right?"

"I'm not following you."

"Bobby and Axel showed up and asked for your help to find a gaming sheet, yes?"

Agnes looked confused momentarily, then she said slowly, "Yes-yes, that's right. I wonder what made me forget that! I really should have told you; I'm so sorry I forgot!" There was hesitation in her voice. "Who told you anyway?"

"Ah, I have my ways of finding out things. After all, I am a detective. But can I know what happened next?"

"Well, it's just as you mentioned: they asked if we had seen it just before Emily served the coffee. We all then left the kitchen and searched everywhere for it. Emily and I searched the study while the boys were— were, actually, I don't know where they were searching, but after I found it under some books, I passed it to Axel in the hallway. They went straight up, and we went back into the kitchen, me to sample my cookies. That's all, I think. The rest you already know. I really am sorry once more."

She had withheld that from us deliberately. Anybody would have known! But why? That was in her favour; now, we know someone else could have slipped into the kitchen in all the confusion without being seen. Maybe even Axel or Bobby, but they both seemed unlikely murderers. Was she protecting someone? Did *she* know who did it?

"It's all right. I forget many things myself!"

"Is that all?"

"Actually, I wanted to know Miss Riker's and Miss Flannel's addresses. I would like to ask them a few questions."

"I don't know their addresses but I can ring them up and set up a meeting here if you like."

"Can we visit them instead? I think it would be ideal to have it at either Evelyn's or Debbrah's house for a change."

"I'll ask. I left my hand phone upstairs. Please wait here."

She headed back upstairs.

"Stay here! I'll be back," said Andrew urgently.

"Where are you going?" I asked, but he was already venturing deeper into the house; the labyrinth of the ground floor enveloping him.

So, wait I did. For a few minutes too. Finally, he came back. But I didn't have time to ask him anything because Agnes returned as well.

"I've called them, but only Debbrah answered. I guess Evelyn's not in. Anyway, she said tomorrow morning is a good time, at her place. So, I'll check with Evelyn later today and keep you posted."

"Thank you very much. We're actually waiting for James and Audrey. They should be back soon."

"I wouldn't if I were you," she said suddenly. "James is in a bad mood these few days. And *nobody* likes him when he's in a hot temper. If he finds you here waiting for him, he might feel that you're hounding him. Then, you'll never get anything out of him."

"Well, what should we do then? I'd really like to talk to them as soon as possible."

"You could talk to Audrey first. She doesn't mind."

"For this particular case, I'd like to speak to them together, not individually. Could we perhaps wait in the study? Then, after they return, you could put it nicely to James, and hopefully we can get it done."

"I'll try, but I can't guarantee anything. I'll inform you after I talk to him."

So, we hid ourselves in the study and when I was finally sure we were alone, I asked Andrew about his little escapade.

"I had to ask Emily about what Agnes said. You remember, she said they searched the library *together*."

"And what did Emily say?"

"Well, at first, she kept on apologizing and slapping herself on her forehead for forgetting to tell us the first time round, then when I finally calmed her down, she thought a little while, then said 'yes'. She *was* with Agnes the whole time."

"So they're each other's alibis . . . . coupled with the fact that they actually found the game sheet, they seem innocent to me."

"Lots of things could prove otherwise, Philipps. No, it's still not time to mark anybody off."

"So, now what?"

"We do as we told Agnes; we wait."

"Sounds good to me," I chuckled as I selected the 'Computing Skills for Dummies' book. *Finally.*

The next time I checked my watch, I realized that an hour had gone by already. It was now 3.10pm.

"How long do we have to wait?" I grumbled. I realized then that Andrew wasn't reading, but was busy scribbling away in his pocket notebook.

"Patience, my friend."

""What are you doing?"

"Making notes. I can't remember everything, you know . . . ."

"For the whole past hour?"

"It's not just notes. I'm already starting to picture what happened that night. I'm writing that in too, just to see if it makes sense."

"Tell me. We can do it together."

"And you wouldn't have learned anything! Where's the fun in that?"

"How do I learn if I don't even know where to begin?" I protested.

"Look now. You and I were given the same information at the same time. Start there I suppose. It's what I did." He had still been scribbling.

"But I'm not a detec—"

The door opened after two consecutive sharp knocks and Agnes came in without waiting for an answer.

"I've spoken to them. They're home already and they said they'll be with you soon. They just need to freshen up."

"Thank you." His notebook and pen were nowhere in sight.

Before I knew it, the couple was down, seated opposite us, pleasantries exchanged almost mechanically.

"Thank you for meeting us. It's of utmost importance."

"We understand," said Audrey.

"First, James, can you tell us a little about yourself?"

"Most certainly. I am a medical doctor by profession. I now work in the biggest general hospital in town as an eye specialist. I—"

"Eye specialist? I thought public hospitals were meant for general practitioners only."

"Oh, they don't care if you're a specialist or not. You get the same pay as a general practitioner! That's why I actually wanted to move off with Audrey and Bobby to some bigger city with private hospitals. There isn't any in this town, you know."

"Oh, honey, let's not talk about that now, ok? It's not a good time," Audrey said.

"Yes, yes, anyway, I come from North Samaria. I'm not sure if you already know this, but Audrey's parents come from my hometown. Coincidence, right?"

"Oh, interesting!"

"And, uh, what else is there to know about me?"

"Hmm, maybe you can tell us about what happened that night. Your version of it."

"Well, I remember after dinner, we went back into our room. I checked the clock; it was eight twenty I think. I brushed my teeth and had a quick shower before indulging in my medical reference encyclopaedias. I had quite a few rare cases to deal with."

"And you, Mrs. Tholson?"

"We went up together, but while he was showering, I was at my dressing table, applying some, uh, moisturizers and cleansers and lotions. I do that every night. Then, I started reading the week's edition of Women's Weekly till I dozed off."

"And the next morning, news reached us that she was dead. I think it was Emily who woke us up and told us the tragic news," said James.

"Yes, poor Aunt Geraldine."

"James, I heard from Dr. Marion that the autopsy was done in the hospital you work in. Were you involved in that?"

"No, I wasn't. They told me I was a relative and shouldn't have done it. I have the report though, if you want to see it."

"No, I don't, thank you. But can you brief me through it?"

"Strychnine. The poison that killed her. Drugs and poisons are not my specialties, but I do know that it causes loss of control of muscles, as in excessive convulsions and contractions and it kills by affecting one's respiratory muscles to the point of asphyxia. Asphyxia is dying from lack of oxygen. But the autopsy estimates the poison was ingested around midnight, which seems to clash with the general perception. I, for one, understand that she drank the coffee around nine."

"We did discuss that with Dr. Marion, and—"

"Oh, you did! I see," he said, a little offended.

"Well, he only told us a little, but we agreed on something like the dosage of strychnine could have been so little that the symptoms didn't show until later, much later. Is that possible?"

"Possible, yes, but highly unlikely. Perhaps, the autopsy is wrong after all."

"Yes, maybe. Anyway, do either of you know what is in her will?"

They both just shook their heads as expected.

"She never mentioned it. I know it's with her lawyer, but we're all left in the dark, so much so that I'm beginning to doubt she even wrote a will . . . ." Audrey said. "But if what I think is correct, then her assets should be divided equally among my siblings and me and my mother."

"There isn't a chance that she might have left it all to your mother?"

"Oh, I doubt it. She's intelligent; intelligent enough to realize that my mother, being of old age, wouldn't need much money. No, I'm quite sure she would have divided it equally if not even more for us than for my mother."

"How much do you expect?"

"I don't know, but I imagine quite enough for James to start his own clinic. Finally, right James? It's what you've always wanted!"

James blushed a little, then stuttered, "Well, that would be nice . . . ."

"Alright, anyway, can you tell me what sort of person your aunt was?"

"She, oh, she was a little, um, ok, *very* stingy. I've always known her as someone who cared more about her dollars and dimes than about us. She didn't hate us; that's for sure, but she could have loved more. That's . . . . all I'm saying," said Audrey.

"No comments," said James.

"I think that's all actually. Just to be clear, both of you, having gone upstairs after dinner, didn't come down again that night?"

"No, we didn't," said James.

"Thank you once more and have a good evening."

"Wait, Mr. Sommers, Mr. Philipps, won't you stay for dinner? I heard we're having cold chicken served with fresh garden lettuce, and some pudding for dessert. It'll be delicious, trust me. Betty's a great cook."

"That's very generous of you. Thank you. What time will that be?"

"Are you in a rush? I see you have a car. It's normally at half past seven, but we could have it a little earlier if you—"

"No, no, seven thirty's just fine. Thank you."

"Have you spoken to our son and Axel?"

"Yes, we have."

"It's only five now; do you have any plans?" said Audrey.

"No, actually. But I might want to have a few words with Betty. We missed her the past few times we came here."

"She's probably in the kitchen just about to prepare dinner. You know the way, don't you?"

"Yes, I'll go now. The both of you can go and, uh, rest if you like. These sort of things are normally tiring I understand."

"Oh, no, I'm fine. Besides, it's rude not to entertain our guests," she said, smiling.

"Well, honey, suit yourself, but I think I'll be upstairs," said James.

And so he left, smiling or scowling I wasn't sure, leaving three of us behind. Not long after that, Andrew excused himself, saying he intended to have a word with Betty. And then there were two.

"So, Mr. Philipps, what do you do for a living?"

"Please, call me Tony. I was a lecturer in the University of Deweira teaching English Literature when I was younger, but now I just write novels for the fun of it."

"Oh, how exciting! I was under the impression you were Mr. Sommer's colleague from young. A fellow detective or an officer maybe."

"Nothing that fantastic! I'm merely his companion now, Mrs. Tholson."

"Please, call me Audrey," she said. "We have so much time before dinner, and I was thinking maybe we do something out of the norm. Radical, so to say!"

"Like what?"

"I know my husband and probably everyone else in the family would be appalled, but I'm going to take out the old mahjong set."

"But I don't know how to play!"

"So, I'll teach you. Then, we can teach Mr. Sommers, and I'll get Axel to fill up the last spot, and we'll play till dinner!"

"Hmm, that does sound interesting . . . ."

"Good! Wait here!"

She retrieved a large leather case from one of the numerous drawers in the room and placed it with a thud on the table. She opened the case like a magician would open a cupboard with a hundred swords driven into it, right before saying something like "Tadah! The girl is alive!". She unfolded a very large piece of thin, white, translucent paper and covered the study table with it.

"Mahjong paper. For the pieces later."

I said nothing but watched on, curiosity building up little by little. Then, she emptied the pieces onto the mahjong paper carefully. There were many of them, too many to count. This was the first time I'd seen a mahjong set, and now, curiosity evolved into excitement, and excitement had many questions to ask!

"That's quite a lot of pieces. How many are there all together?"

"I think there are a hundred and thirty-six tiles, including jokers."

"It's a game meant for four people, right? What if you have more or less players?"

"If we had more, we'd have to take turns and if less, we'll do what I'm about to do: get others!"

All the while, she was flipping the pieces so that they were the right side up, and I got slightly dizzy trying to absorb and understand what the pieces meant. Each piece, no smaller than an average eraser, had either a Chinese character on it, pictures or dots. And they were all very colourful. I tried to establish a pattern or a rule by which the game could possibly be based on, but I failed . . . . miserably. It was simply too complicated, and Audrey proved me right when she started to teach me.

"Go on. Take a tile. Don't be shy."

I selected one with a Chinese character on it. I'm no linguist, but I was quite sure that was a seven.

"That's a nine." Oops.

Then, she started teaching me, the details of which I shan't bother to record here (partly because I've forgotten). Suffice to say it was very confusing, something about drawing and discarding pieces and securing a complete set comprising of melds and a head to achieve victory. See what I meant? Just believe me when I say it's confusing. Andrew came in then.

"Mr. Sommers, you're just in time! I've just about finished teaching Tony how to play. Tony, you teach him while I go get Axel."

She left before I could say anything. Andrew stared hard at me.

"Mahjong? Tony? What is this, a rebellion?"

"Don't ask questions. Sit. I need to teach you before I forget."

But by the time Andrew had settled down and understood that we were merely killing time before dinner, Audrey had reappeared with Axel.

"Good evening, detectives. I see you've decided to learn mahjong. I'm surprised I must say." Axel's tone was a mixture of sombreness and cheerfulness at the same time. He was wearing a very exotic shade of yellow. Brightened the room immediately.

"So, how are you doing so far?"

"Not very good, I'm afraid," I said. Huge understatement.

"No matter. Axel, please teach them. You'd do a much better job than I would!" said Audrey.

"It's my pleasure to."

So, he taught us. For a whole half hour. And I was only a little better off than before I set foot into this house for the first time! Then, the game began, the details of which I shall again avoid recording. But I will tell you this: Andrew won one round! Until now I still don't know how he did it, but I insist it was by pure luck.

"Oops! It's already seven twenty! Come on! Help me pack up. Punctuality for meals is greatly treasured in this household," said Audrey.

We literally threw the tiles into the case which Audrey hurriedly replaced in the drawer and tumbled out of the room, Axel tripping a little. We bumped into Agnes just outside. She was just on her way to the dining room.

"Oh, hello! You're still here?" she asked, clearly surprised, but not in a disgusted manner.

'Yes, I invited them to stay for dinner," said Audrey.

"Good; I would have done so first had it not slipped my mind! Come on then. We're a little late already."

Dinner With The Farells

So, the five of us trooped into the dining room. And, yes, we were the last ones there. I had a quick glance at everybody else seated and observed their facial expressions: Alvin's was friendly, Bobby's was a little too chubby to have had displayed any visible expression, Gina's was a surprised one that transformed rapidly into poorly concealed disgust and James' was expressionless. Emily, who was serving dishes onto the dining table, paused momentarily before saying, "I'll get two more dinner sets."

Eventually, we were all seated, me beside Andrew who was beside Agnes, beside Gina, followed by either Audrey or James (can't remember by now), then the other one, then Bobby, Axel, Alvin and back to me.

"Orange coolers for everyone?" asked Emily when she had set two plates of chicken and three plates of lettuce on the table.

Everybody said 'yes' in unison, followed by 'thank you'. And thus, the meal went underway. Audrey was right indeed; the food was delicious! The chicken was simply lip-smacking and the lettuce was as crispy as fried bread crumbs. The perfect blend, washed down by the cooler was ecstasy. But just as I was swallowing my second mouthful of the liquid, Axel spat and sputtered, spewing orange cooler from his mouth behind his chair. His face was all red and he coughed violently, one hand clasped around his throat and the other gripped his chair for support. Everybody stopped chewing or cutting or whatever they were doing and fixed their eyes on Axel.

Finally, he turned around to face us, his face a shade of red slightly less deep than beetroot.

"Ugh! Most bitter thing I've ever tasted!" he said, lifting his almost-full glass of cooler and examining its contents. Naturally, everybody shifted their focus onto the glass, but it was hard to see much in the dim light. "Has anyone tasted their coolers? Is it supposed to be this bitter?" he asked.

I was the first to say mine was sweet and was quickly followed by the others at the table. Andrew thrust his hand up suddenly to command silence in the increasingly chaotic situation.

"Axel, please pass me your glass." Axel did. Andrew dipped a teaspoon into it and scooped some liquid out from the bottom of the glass. Upon closer inspection, he released an 'Ah!'. Everybody, myself included, had puzzled faces and exchanged curious glances with each other.

"Everybody, stop drinking your coolers. Axel's has been spiked with strychnine!"

Unrestrained ejaculations of shocked noises echoed around the room. I myself was feeling slightly nauseous. I had consumed two mouthfuls of that drink for goodness sake!

"And what the hell is strychnine?" shouted Axel.

"Strychnine? You mean the poison that killed Aunt Geraldine?" asked Agnes, a very worried expression splattered on her face.

"Yes, exactly that!" said Andrew.

"How do you know?" How did it get there?" James asked.

"I know because the crystals haven't dissolved. They're here on the spoon. Strychnine crystals can only be dissolved in ethanol, if I'm not wrong. Strychnine is very, very bitter, and I think Axel just proved me right! But how it got there is a very good question indeed . . . ." he said, looking round at everybody. "Axel, did you swallow any?"

"No, I spat it all out!"

"Are you sure?"

"Yes."

"Just to be sure, go to the wash room and gargle thoroughly with water. Then, I need you to try to vomit. However little is fine. Just in case."

Axel left the table hurriedly without saying anything.

"But what about the rest of us? I'm sure we've all swallowed some!" said Alvin, panic rising in his voice.

"Don't worry. None of you complained about bitterness, right? I think his drink is the only one with the poison. And also, check your drinks for any crystals like these." He lifted his spoon. "They're colourless, but quite easy to spot."

Everybody did, but nobody produced any crystals.

"If you're still uncomfortable, change your drinks to plain water; you'd be able to taste the bitterness immediately and spot the crystals with relative ease."

"That's a good idea," said Audrey. "Emily! Could you please clear all these coolers and get us plain water instead?"

"Right away, ma'am," said Emily, who had joined the commotion a short while back.

"Please, finish your meal. I would like to speak with Axel now. Philipps, are you coming with me or staying?"

The cold chicken was hard to pass up, but this was very much more important.

"Yes, I'm following you," I said, getting up. "The food was delicious. Compliments to Betty! Enjoy the food." And we left, all of them staring hard at us. I wish I knew what went on in there after we left.

We caught up with Axel just as he exited the restroom. His face was a little pale, but otherwise, he was alright.

"Did you vomit anything out?"

"Yes, a little. But all the same, I'm quite sure I didn't swallow any."

"Alright, Axel, could we—"

"Wait, wait. Come! Follow me. I need to tell you something urgently."

Without further hesitation, he led us upstairs to the room beside the lounge. It was quite empty and unfurnished except for the bare necessities.

"This is the second guestroom. I used to stay here before I moved into Bobby's room. Nobody will disturb us here."

He leaned against the wall and, motioning with his hand, said, "Sit if you like. This will be quick, so I'm standing."

"No, no, we'll stand too. What is it you wanted to say?" asked Andrew.

My heart was racing again. Even before, when we first spoke to him, he was so conservative and now, he was volunteering information! And after what happened, I knew it had to be important.

"The poison in my cup tonight? I know who did it."

"You do? Who?"

"But if I tell you, you mustn't go to the police."

"But you almost just died! If you think you know who did it, then why not get the police?"

"I don't think; I know. And because . . . . the person who did it is Mr. Tholson, Bobby's father."

My mouth dropped open wide. James? What?

"What makes you so sure?"

"On the 8th, the night she died, we, Bobby and I, were downstairs, remember? Searching everywhere. And, I saw Mr. Tholson downstairs out of the corner of my eye, something I believe he didn't tell you, right? I saw him near the kitchen. And then, it all happened so quickly: she had been murdered! When the police came with their questions and you with yours, I couldn't accept the truth. I couldn't accept that he had done it!"

"How do you know he had done it? Surely you did not see him actually place the poison in the cup?"

"You're right; I didn't see him actually commit the crime. But put two and two together, come on, you're a detective, and you'll see that what I'm suggesting *must* be the truth!"

"And why didn't you tell anybody?"

"I decided to let it pass; it was better for all of us that way. I don't care if Geraldine was dead or not, and I feel it serves her right too now that she is. I was just going to go home and keep this to myself. No one need ever know. So, I said nothing."

"Until now."

"Because he just tried to kill me!"

"Did he even know you noticed him that night?"

"At first, I thought not, and Bobby didn't see him either, but now I guess we all know he knew!"

"So what do you want us to do now?"

"Now, you know the truth. Go ahead! Tell everybody, then leave. You've done enough here. Consider this case closed. Then, I can finally leave this place. All I wanted to be is home, but I got stuck in this nightmare, wondering what to do! All my options seemed like no options at all! Tell me, what would you have done if you were me? Destroy a family over a dead woman, or hold silence, wondering when I could go back?"

"And if we do tell everybody, wouldn't you want us to tell the police as well?"

"No, please don't. He's still a good man even if he did just try to kill me, and like I said, he's got a family here. His wife! Bobby! They would be so devastated! And anyway, I'm still alive!"

"But Geraldine is not!"

"Yes! Fine! She's dead! But by arresting him, can you bring her back to life? He tried to kill me because he felt threatened; but if I leave, everyone will be safe. They may condemn him, but there's no need for him to be prosecuted by the law. Give it time. Maybe, everything will settle down. He is, after all, part of the family."

"You expect me to just close one eye, and let him off scot-free? Where is the justice in that? And what about the police? They *will* need answers."

"Well, I've thought about that, actually. The police look up to you and respect what you say. No one else will get hurt if you just say the case is closed. Convince them that you've done all you can, and failed to come up with any solid results, or just say it was after all, a suicide. They'll believe you, trust me."

"But not only would that be wrong in the eyes of the law, it would tarnish my reputation!"

"You finally showed your true colours. It's about your reputation! It's always about reputation, isn't it? So much for solving the case for the sake of justice and all that rubbish you spewed out the first time you came. Honestly, nobody here believes you could solve it, and you wouldn't have had it not been for me or for tonight's incident."

"But—"

"Listen: if you choose to pursue this matter, I can always deny having said anything!"

"But I'm a witness!" I said.

"I don't mean to be rude, but I sincerely doubt your testimony will carry much weight."

"And why not?"

"Are you really that naïve? Simply because you're on his side, his accomplice! Anybody would be convinced that you planned this out together. Plus, look at me. An innocent boy who had his words *twisted*!"

"Please, stop this childish arguing! Axel, all that we do is for your best, but rest assured all these will stay among the three of us unless you permit otherwise."

"Yes, that's the way it should be."

"But you'll have to find some way to stay alive till you get home. He might try again."

"I'll be fine, don't worry. And if anything happens to me, you'll know who to look for. And if I'm dead, *don't* let him off." He smiled, clearly joking.

"This is not a game, Axel! You must be careful."

"Ok, ok. But what are *you* going to do?"

"I need a little more time before I do anything."

"For what?"

"I need to go home and think things through. It's not that I don't trust you, but I need to be sure. It's the way these things should be handled."

"Fine, but, like I said, you'll see that I'm right. Just be sure to do it quickly. I want to go home as soon as I can. I'm sick of this place."

* * *

I was still a bit dizzy from the sudden revelation of knowledge, so dizzy and blur that I can't really recall what happened next. Everything happened so quickly. The next thing I remembered was us getting into Andrew's car, the 'goodbyes' having already been said, apparently headed for home. It was a dark night; a night sky without stars, and a hidden moon.

"Wha—What really happened? Is the case solved?"

"Yes. But not the way you think it to be."

"What do you mean?"

"Put it simply: just one more day and I'll be sure."

"What's there to be sure of? James did it. End of story."

"How can you just take Axel's word for it? And he didn't even see James actually do it!"

"But what else can we go on? We have nothing!"

"Ah, *you* have nothing; I, on the other hand, know what I'm doing. Just one more day. Then, I'll be sure. By tomorrow night, this case would have been a thing of the past."

"What are we doing tomorrow then? During the day?"

"We do as planned. We'll have a word with Mr. Buckling, then with Debbrah and Evelyn. I just need to convince myself fully."

Mr. Buckling

So, the next morning, we drove down to 7 Browning Street, and entered unit 3A-7-2 of the office building.

"Good morning, welcome to Buckling & Hampton Advocates & Solicitors. Who are you looking for?" said the receptionist. She was a fair-skinned Indian with very sunken eyes.

"Good morning. We're looking for Mr. Buckling. We have a ten o'clock appointment with him," said Andrew.

"You are, err, Mr. Sommers and Mr. Philipps, yes?" she asked, reading our names off her desktop screen.

"Yes."

"Please go straight in; he's expecting you," she said as she pointed at the door on her left with one hand and picked up the phone with the other. "Your ten o'clock is here, sir."

We knocked and entered a large, well-furnished and decorated room. It was so strikingly in contrast to the waiting room that I felt I had just walked into another dimension, my eyes enjoying the beauty of such a working environment. Mr. Buckling looked in his late thirties, a very serious expression portrayed on his face. I didn't like his eyes; too cruel in my opinion, and his lips: a sinister sight to behold!

"Good morning, Mr. Buckling."

"Good morning. How can I help you?"

"I understand Miss Farell has arranged this appointment on our behalf but allow me to formally introduce myself. I'm Mr. Sommers, the detective involved in the case of Miss Geraldine Stevenson's, your client's, unfortunate death, and this is Mr. Philipps, my assistant."

"Yes, I know who you are. Miss Agnes Farell called, saying that you would like to know the contents of the late Miss Stevenson's will. I'm afraid our firm has very strict rules governing the disclosure of such information by which we all have to abide. But considering your position and the capacity you're in, I can however, outline briefly the contents of her will on one condition: you may not disclose or relay this information to any member of the household, regardless of whether they stand to gain directly or otherwise from the knowledge of such information. By agreeing, you are obliged to use the information for the sole purpose of solving the case. Leave me to officially read the will at a time that is convenient to them. Do we have a deal?"

"Of course."

I, for one, was still busy trying to understand all that he had just meticulously regurgitated.

"Alright then." He withdrew a leather-cover notebook from his drawer, and read out, "She has donated a quarter of her monetary assets to charity, saying that she wanted to do a good deed in the hopes that she might find peace in knowing her money was well invested. The remainder was to be distributed evenly among her three nephew and nieces. Her shares and other investments she willed to her sister, Gina. The house and land on which it was built is also left in its entirety to Gina to live in and do as she pleases. Any miscellaneous belongings of hers, excluding furniture, may be sold and the money given to Bobby, whom she treated like her own grandson, except for her prized coin collection which she hopes Bobby will take good care of. That's all there is. I cannot disclose estimated amounts of all her possessions, however."

"Yes, we understand. According to my sources, nobody in the family has even the slightest hint of what's in that will, correct?"

"Well, *I* haven't said anything to anybody except to the both of you today, but if Miss Stevenson had spoken out of her own free will when she was alive, then it doesn't concern me. I can't stop that; it's her choice."

"What was the time period between her death and the time she made the will?"

"Five years approximately, but I should think that most of the details are still relevant. It's not like she's been making any risky investments or losing chunks of money for nothing. Besides, she made her first will many years back when my father was still working. Now, he's retired, and since I've taken over she's only altered it once. And that's the will that's currently in effect. Her old will and this new one have essentially the same assets, but the distribution is different, of course. And again, I am disallowed from disclosing in what way they are actually different."

"Yes, yes. Thank you for your time. You have been of great help to us."

"You're welcome. Have a nice day."

Debbrah Rikers &
Evelyn Flannel

When we had left the building, I said, "I hope you found what you were looking for, but to me, all this is just a waste of time! Where to next?"

"Why are you in such a hurry to finish this? The finer details should not be overlooked. Agnes called me last night, saying that we could drop by at Debbrah's place for morning coffee while going through the questions."

"What time?"

"Ten thirty."

"Then, we're late!"

"Yes, I know, so hurry!"

We got into his car, and before I could even manage my seatbelt, he had shot off. At a speed much faster than I had ever seen him in. Hmm . . . . punctuality *was* that important to him. We went along roads I wasn't familiar with, and just as I thought we were lost, he said, "We're here!", the car jerking to a complete halt, throwing me a few inches forward.

"Ten forty-three! We're *so* late."

"Relax, relax; it's just a few minutes!"

"Sshhh, stop talking," he hissed as he rang the doorbell.

We were at 17 Quickman Road, evidently Debbrah's house as suggested by a small wooden sign that had embossed on it the word 'Rikers'. It was a simple terrace house, with lovely flower pots in the garden. So, this was what the average retired person's house looked like. An elderly woman opened the door.

"Hello there! Are you Mr. Sommers and, uh—" She had quite obviously forgotten my name.

"Good morning. Yes, I'm Andrew Sommers and he's Tony Philipps."

"Ah . . . . Philipps! *That* was it. I'm Debbrah Rikers. You can call me Deb. Come on in!"

"Thank you."

"Eve?" she said when inside. "They're here. Could you get the coffee? I'll take them to the dining table."

We hung our coats and hats and followed her through the white-walled, country-cottage themed interior to a homely wooden table set against a wall with many photo frames on it. Old memories, no doubt. Just as we sat down, we were joined by another old woman, but this one with locks of golden hair instead of white. She was carrying in her hands a tray with cups and a pot of coffee. Déjà vu set in, and I pictured that that must have been how it was when Geraldine died. What an eerie coincidence indeed! I looked at Andrew but he was as calm as ever. I stared hard at Eve, but she had neither sinister nor murderous look in her eyes.

"Good morning. I'm Eve. I hope you like coffee," she said as she set the tray on the table.

"Good morning. I'm Andrew Sommers and this is Tony. Coffee's great, but we won't stay long. We just need to ask a few questions."

"Please go ahead."

"Can we have your account of what happened after dinner the night Geraldine was poisoned?"

"Well, we were playing mahjong. I'm sure you know that already. We had coffee at nine, an unusual beverage to have at such a time, but for whatever reason, we had it. If we had known that the poison was going to be administered that way, we would never have let her near the coffee . . . . what a tragic incident indeed," said Deb. Eve put her hand on her shoulder and offered a weak smile.

"Whose idea was it to have the coffee?" asked Andrew.

"Hmmm, I actually don't know . . . . Eve?" said Debbrah.

"No, I don't remember either."

"But I think it was her own, I mean Geraldine's idea to have coffee. Something about not falling asleep during Mahjong; she *is* a fanatic!" said Debbrah.

"Alright, what happened next?"

"Then, we went home slightly past midnight I think, completely oblivious to the fact that that was the last time we'd ever see her. We're not as close as family, but at this age, friends *are* family!" Eve said, tears rolling down her cheeks.

"It's ok; it's fine. Take your time. Cry if you must. Tears bring healing; they were created to fight the pain; fight the sorrow." But after saying all that, the two women had stopped crying already.

"We're alright; you may continue. Oh, it's just the tears come every now and then, and it's so much more scary to know she was poisoned right beside us! Death had never felt so close before!" said Deb.

"How long have you known her?"

"A good many years I should say! Though I can't be exact. We knew her since she moved in a long time ago, though it seems just like yesterday . . . ." Eve said, nostalgia kicking in, casting a very hollow look in her eyes.

"How often do you visit her for mahjong or whatever else?"

"As and when we felt up to it. Sometimes, once a week, sometimes more often, other times less, though it wasn't always mahjong. Bridge was more common. One of us would call the other two, and *voila*, a gathering is planned! That simple!" Eve said.

"Yes, I forgot to ask earlier, who poured out the coffee that night? Did Emily serve it in cups already? Or did she leave it in a pot and you had to pour it out yourselves?"

"I think Gina poured it out for all of us the first time, then subsequent refills we managed ourselves," Deb said.

"Was there anything unusual about Geraldine that night?"

"Yes; her luck! She was on fire, winning round after round, leaving little for the three of us! But in terms of physical appearance or behaviour, not much. I'm not sure though. Deb?" said Eve.

"She said something about the coffee, something vague, but I wasn't really paying attention, so I don't know."

"What sort of person was she?"

"I think we're not in any position to talk about that; we're not close enough to her to provide you with anything creditable. You should speak with any of the other family members or at least, Axel, because he stays there and would know her better than we would."

"But you've known her for so many years!"

"Yes, but we only know her when it comes to Mahjong or bridge! Oh, what am I saying! I mean that we know only that side of her. We wouldn't know how she is like at home, in her room for example, what she does behind everybody's back, what she does in secret and so on. That is, after all, what you're after, isn't it?" said Debbrah.

Eve merely nodded in agreement with Debbrah.

"Yes, thank you. I've no more questions. Can you come by this evening at five to the Stevenson Mansion? We would like to clear this business once and for all and it's only appropriate if you be there when we do it."

"We'd love to. See you tonight then and we're glad we were of help to you," said Debbrah.

The Calm Before
The Storm

"**N**ow what?" I asked, tired of never knowing what we were doing next till Andrew told me. I was honestly sick of hearing myself repeat that question.

"We go back to the Farells'."

"What for? I thought you said the meeting was tonight."

"I need to tidy up a few things."

"You seem pretty confident, don't you? Well, I hope when the meeting comes tonight, you won't embarrass yourself or me."

"I won't because I've solved it!"

"Have you really now? I feel we've been going back and forth and that we're not getting anywhere."

"What you feel differs greatly from what I feel, and conversely, the truth . . . ."

I sat in silence, appalled by his egoism and over-confidence. I may be stupid, but I'm smart enough to know he hadn't solved it yet. How could he when we were given the same details? I wasn't even close to drawing a conclusion! Too many variables, too many possibilities, too many ways the murder could have gone wrong! We reached their house then, and my thoughts were disrupted.

"Could we please speak to Bobby?" Andrew asked Sebastian when we were inside.

"Yes, I'll inform him."

James emerged suddenly from the kitchen, holding an apple in his hand.

"Oh, hi! Just helping myself to some fruit."

"Hi, we're looking for Bobby. Sebastian went up to get him."

"Alright, listen! I need to tell you this; it's important. Everybody in this household agreed to never mention this to anyone outside the family, but I think you should know. It would be unfair if we withheld this from you. Alvin is not actually my brother-in-law in blood. He's not biologically related to Gina, Agnes, or Audrey."

I was stunned and at a loss of words.

"You mean he was adopted?" I said.

"Yes! I heard that Gina couldn't give birth at first, so she adopted Alvin, but a year later she had Audrey, then Agnes. But they've always treated him like real family. I just . . . . feel you ought to know, whether it's relevant or not to recent happenings. Don't tell anybody I said this."

"Don't feel guilty; you're merely confirming what I've already suspected to be true," Andrew said.

My heart stopped beating a second time in the past minute. Andrew knew? Andrew knew and didn't tell me?

"But how did you know?" asked James.

"The way your mother-in-law phrased something, though she never meant to—" said Andrew, but heavy footsteps were heard coming from the top of the stairs just then. James hurriedly picked up his apple which he had earlier set down on the side table and started up the stairs, flashing his right index finger over his lips hastily at us before removing it and turning away. Halfway up the stairs, he muttered something to Bobby, who nodded upon hearing it, and vanished from sight.

"Hello, detectives. How can I help you?" Bobby asked when he reached the last step.

"Bobby, I need to ask you something in private. I need to confirm my suspicions."

"Sure. I suppose it would be in the study?"

I started walking towards the hallway leading to the study but Andrew grabbed my shoulder hard, and whispered in my ear.

"It's really important that I ask him alone. Keep an eye; make sure nobody eavesdrops. I'll be out soon."

So, I reluctantly watched them head towards the study, then sat down on the sofa in the living room where I could see if anybody was near the study. I was half curious, half furious, partly because I had fallen so far behind in the case. It was as if Andrew was an Oxford graduate and I, only a kindergarten student trying to tap into the somewhat fantastic but inexplicable solution to the puzzle and Andrew knew the answer and was baiting me along with a carrot on a stick! I felt stupid and left out, if not betrayed as well. Maybe I should never have come along. I did so to learn, not to end up frustrated the way I was now. And let me tell you, there was nothing more frustrating than being so close to the answer, but falling short just when I needed myself not to.

I sat alone, fuming, desperately trying to piece the puzzle, desperately trying to make good of myself.

Why? Why was I so blind? Why couldn't I get it done? The fragments of the case swirled in my mind, almost as if they were bobbing up and down in a cauldron of opaque goo, appearing for the first second, then gone for the next.

Too many people downstairs during murder . . . . coffee and cookies . . . . game sheet . . . . Emily served the drinks . . . . Gina poured the coffee . . . . mahjong . . . . Alvin . . . . James . . . . alright, it was too much! Who did it? *How* did he do it? The murder seemed impossible! It seemed to happen completely by chance!

While pondering all these, Andrew came out, hand on Bobby's shoulder.

"We'll see you in the evening then," Andrew said to Bobby as he rejoined me at the sofa.

"I'd ask what happened, but I don't care anymore," I said, my frustration surfacing.

"Come now, why are you so down? This is a time to celebrate!"

"And why the heck would we do that?"

"You are too pessimistic, my friend. Come with me."

"And where are we going now?" I asked sceptically.

"To my place. I'm going to write everything down . . . . But before we go, look over there," he said as he pointed to the wall behind me.

I did.

"What is it?" I asked, turning to face Andrew again.

"Now, I want you to tell me how many fingers I put up while your back was facing me."

"How would I know how many fingers? My back was turned. You said it yourself!"

"Exactly! That's the way this murder was done!"

"How? I don't understand what this has to do with the murder."

"It has *everything* to do with it! Come now. I'll reveal all to you . . . ."

Revelation

At four forty-five, we knocked on the door to
the Stevenson Mansion, I hoped, for the last
time. I took a sombre glance at the wooden
walls of the interior and felt the stench of death and
deceit mask the once joyful fragrance that permeated
the house. No. Not anymore. There was only despair
now, and I wondered if the family had really gotten
over the death of Gina's husband to begin with. Or
was it just a façade? Was this recent murder the logical
follow-up to the incident that stained these walls so
many years back? Was it the mansion or the residents?
When anybody smiled in these hallways, were they
sincere? Or was it merely a trained facial gesture that
bore no meaning?

But now was not the time to ask or answer such
questions. It was merely the time for reckoning. And,
so, we were all assembled in the spacious drawing room,
tension hung in the air like a disease, straining all faces
but one: Andrew's, who seemed to enjoy watching

everybody at their tenterhooks. I looked around at everybody, hardly able to believe that one of them had indeed committed murder.

"Well, we've all gathered here as you've requested. What did you want to say?" asked Agnes.

"I'm here to deliver as promised."

"You mean to say you know who murdered her?" asked James. His eyes bulging out in disbelief.

"Yes, that's correct. But before I mention any names, I'm going to give a brief account of what happened that night. Since we are all quite sure that her death had nothing to do with what she had for dinner, I'll just start from after the meal. Now, Axel, Bobby, Audrey and James went upstairs, while Alvin went out to buy cigarettes. Agnes and Emily were in the kitchen, baking and washing respectively. Geraldine, Gina, Debbrah and Evelyn were playing mahjong. Refreshments were served at around nine. Coffee in a pot, together with the cookies Agnes baked. But just before that, Bobby and Axel came down in search of Axel's game sheet, and soon, the two of them, together with Agnes and Emily, searched the whole of downstairs for it. Agnes eventually found it in the library. But around then, Alvin comes home from the store. And it seems James was downstairs too."

"I was not! I never went down stairs after dinner until the next morning! Who told you I went down?" asked James, his voice raised to a threatening decibel.

"Yes, he's right! I was with him in our room the entire night!" said Audrey.

"Ah, but surely you went to the bathroom. Even five minutes would have been more than enough!"

"Well . . . . I did, but—" said Audrey.

"But that doesn't mean I went down! You have no proof!" said James.

"Somebody saw you downstairs that night, Mr. Tholson! And around nine too!"

"Who? Tell me who!"

"That doesn't matter; if you'd please just let me finish."

"Fine! Let's see what you've got!"

"So, there were, in fact, nine people on this floor that night at around nine, excluding Geraldine. Funny how everybody needed to be downstairs just then, isn't it?"

"It's not very funny at all. Get on with it," said James, clearly irritated.

"After all the confusion, I understand Axel and Bobby went back up upon retrieving the game sheet and that Emily served the refreshments. Agnes had gone up around then. But it's unclear when Alvin and James went up as we have no witnesses. And Gina, Deb, Eve and Geraldine were relatively undisturbed and oblivious to their surroundings."

"I went straight up. I told you that the last time we met. I didn't see anybody else," said Alvin.

"I was never downstairs to begin with!" said James.

"Please, gentleman, it doesn't matter once more. Other than you, James, can everybody agree that what I've just outlined so far is the truth?"

There were heads nodding everywhere and a few muttered 'yes's echoing around the room.

"Now, I need all of you to picture this: there were so many people downstairs, but none of them really bumped into each other in the little maze we find ourselves in. And when Alvin went up, he saw nobody on the corridor. And neither did Agnes when she went up. This is of utmost significance. And now, something I think none of you know: Bobby, while in his room, saw every movement at the top of the stairs! He saw who came up, who went down, and when too!"

Everybody was surprised, some with their mouths slightly open.

"Why didn't you say anything about that, dear?" asked Audrey.

"Because I told him not to! He is much safer this way. And it's a good thing he forgot to tell the police too because they would have exposed him with that knowledge and I doubt Bobby would still be alive today. Indeed, Bobby *did* see the murderer that night!"

"No, I didn't!" said Bobby.

"Please let me finish. You just didn't realize you did. Another thing is that I wondered how the poison actually ended up in Geraldine's cup."

"Well, obviously, *somebody* put it in!" said Alvin impatiently.

"But how and when? I mean if somebody had put the poison in the cup before Emily served it, there was a seventy-five percent chance Geraldine could have chosen the wrong cup, and the poison would have been administered to the wrong person. No! The murderer had to be absolutely sure that Geraldine and Geraldine alone consumed the poison. And how would he do that? By making sure the poison ended up in *her* cup. Or at least, make it *look* that way!"

"What do you mean? Are you suggesting I did it? True, I poured the first serving of coffee and handed Geraldine her cup, but I didn't do it! You have to believe me!" said Gina, her voice a little hoarse.

"I don't believe that happened. And why? Because I think you poured out the coffee when the other three were 'shuffling' the tiles. In fact, I'm sure of it. It was the most natural and probable time for you to pour the coffee out. Not during the game itself! So, there was every possibility that one of the three might look up thoughtlessly as so often happens and see you slip in the crystals. The risk was too great! Manageable, but not necessary. No, the murderer did it in a much better way."

"Well, who did put the poison in?" asked Agnes.

"Ah! Axel did!"

And for the second time that night, everybody had their mouths hanging open wide, before turning to stare at Axel. He had been standing by the cupboard, beside Bobby, the whole time and his face was one of utter surprise.

"What? I did it? But how? I never went near her cup that night!" Axel said.

"Yes, I can vouch for that! He was with me the whole night! You have my word he didn't go near her or her cup!" Bobby said.

"Plus, I remember you saying that the murderer had to be absolutely sure of himself. How could I be if I wasn't near her cup?" asked Axel.

"Ah, but I never said *you* were the murderer, Axel!"

"What are you saying? Have you completely lost your mind? First, you say he puts the poison in the cup, then you say he didn't murder her?" said Agnes.

"I told you it was a mistake hiring him from the start! I'm getting the police if you don't leave now!" said James.

"Wait, wait! Let me explain myself. Would you believe it if I told you that Geraldine Stevenson didn't die because of the coffee?" said Andrew, smiling wryly.

"But how can that be?" asked Audrey.

"Are you saying the police *lied* to us?" asked Alvin, a little sarcastically.

"No, not at all. The police reported there was strychnine in one cup which we assumed to be hers. That is the truth."

"So, she drank the poison, but it wasn't fatal; then she dies in the course of her sleep because of some *other* unknown reason?" asked James, his left eyebrow raised slightly.

"Don't be silly! The autopsy says she died of strychnine poisoning. And that, too, is the truth! The only question remaining is how she consumed it!"

"That isn't a question at all! It *was* the coffee!" said Agnes, quite exasperated.

"No, it was not! It was the water in the kettle in the lounge upstairs!"

Then, came the third round of shocked expressions. I was beginning to enjoy this. When Andrew told me all this, I felt the same way. So, surely it was nice to be watching in from the outside now. Maybe, there was an advantage in being his assistant after all.

"You're saying there was poison in the cup of coffee and in the kettle, but she died because of the poison in the kettle?" Audrey asked.

"Yes! Can't you people see what really happened? I believe that there wasn't any poison in her cup on the 8th. There was only poison in the kettle; but even that had to be timed properly to avoid unintended deaths. The poison was placed at a time when only Geraldine could drink it. Quite late, in other words. The real murderer was the last person who went up before Gina and Geraldine. And that person is you, Agnes."

His right index finger pointed right at her, sparking another round of uniform 'huh's and 'what's. All eyes were fixed on her now.

"Oh, so now it's me! You remember, don't you, the time I told you that if you couldn't solve it, not to resort to wild accusations? This is the craziest thing I've heard of!" Agnes said.

"After I explain myself, you will all see it's not crazy at all! You wanted to murder her, but how? So, you decided the best way was poison. You planned for weeks and waited for that night, taking advantage of the mahjong game, of the fact they were going to have coffee! You bring a lot of attention to the game, to the coffee, to the ground floor, anything but to what happens upstairs, the place the murder was actually committed! Then, you bring everybody downstairs, I mean as many people as you could, to confuse things, to make us believe that the important parts were happening here! The game sheet idea was well planned by you and Axel, but Alvin going out at just that time was pure coincidence, coincidence that you used to your advantage! So now, the scene was set. Everybody's focused on downstairs, everybody had a strong alibi, except Alvin, whom you were going to conveniently shift the blame to had things gotten out of hand. By making everybody suspects, you made nobody suspects, complicating the scenario so much that most people, the police for example, would give up and maybe even brand it as suicide! You even dragged yourself into the mess by baking cookies, another nice touch I must say, so as to shift the suspicion away from you. Reverse psychology, eh? You played the role of the most likely murderess since the beginning in the hope that I, Andrew Sommers, would look further for a solution, and there wouldn't have been any! So, Emily was your alibi, and Bobby was Axel's. Part one settled. Part two: spiking the water in the kettle. By baking the cookies, you allowed yourself to be the last one up before Gina and Geraldine. Upon reaching the first floor, you scouted the hallway and quickly established that no one was around to see you and that you were safe, but what you did not know was that Bobby had seen you! He told me you headed in his direction though your room was the other way. He very convincingly but wrongly said that you went into the toilet next to his room."

"And how do you know I didn't?"

"Because I know for a fact that there is a larger, more comfortable bathroom directly beside your room. And logic says that if you went for a shower like you said you did, you'd use the larger one for convenience. The fact that you did not first turned my suspicions towards you. So, I believe that you went, instead, to the lounge to boil the water with the strychnine crystals in it for Geraldine to drink later. Nobody heard you boil the water, and even if they did, they would think nothing of it!"

"It's all good so far, but then how would I have known that my mother wasn't going to drink from that very kettle? Surely, you're not accusing me of attempting murder on my own mother!" she protested.

"Oh, no! But my answer would be weeks of consistent 'research'. You learnt that your aunt had a habit of drinking hot water before she went to bed, a habit no one, especially not your mother, shared. It was still a gamble, but it was one you were willing to bet on. Good thing you won too! Otherwise, your poor mother would have . . . . died."

"That's insane! Nobody in their right mind would do that! And what about Axel? What has he got to do with any of these?" asked Agnes.

"We come to part three: the diversion. You know, you weren't lying when you first told me you didn't slip the poison into the coffee cup. But then again how could you when you, even until now, do not know where your aunt sat that night, thus, not knowing which cup was hers! Since we already understand it was too risky to put the poison before the murder was committed, it had to be placed after the murder was accomplished! And I remember Gina saying she saw Axel look in during the confusion, a seemingly innocent act at that point of time, but now it all becomes clear; Axel looked into the dining room to learn one thing and one thing alone: where Geraldine sat! Of course, which cup the poison was put into may or may not have been important, and I believe in this case it isn't, but you two planned it out so amazingly well that nothing was left to chance! So that's why I said Axel slipped the poison into the coffee cup, but did not murder Geraldine! I believe that you, Axel, simply snuck out of your room before anybody woke up and placed some strychnine crystals into her cup knowing full well that her cup would be left there."

"As fantastic as all that sounds, what if something went wrong? What if, as you suggest, after poisoning two different liquids, Geraldine didn't die? What if she didn't drink the hot water as she usually did?" said Axel.

"Ah! But that's the beauty of this whole plot! Nothing happens! Life goes on as usual until Agnes decides to try again. You see, if Geraldine was still alive in the morning, Emily would have woken her up, then washed the coffee cups, probably not noticing the strychnine. Problem one down the drain. Now all

Agnes had to do was pour away the poisoned water from the kettle before anyone noticed, leaving no clues behind. And, yes, then she would no doubt have tried again and again until she succeeded."

"Do you think my aunt was stupid? Do you think she would have drunk the water if it was bitter from the poison?" asked Agnes.

"Don't forget, she just had coffee. That bitter taste lingered in her mouth. She would have blamed the bitterness on the coffee and not on the water, suspecting nothing at all. Why should she? She completely didn't expect that someone was about to poison her."

"Wait! Who tried to poison Axel that evening then?" asked Audrey.

"Why, Axel himself of course! To shift the suspicion away from himself, and to put the blame on someone else. That someone else was you, Mr. Tholson."

No words did James utter, just a look of pure disbelief on his face.

"You see, that was Axel's biggest mistake. It quickly drew my suspicions towards him; his plan had backfired miserably. Things, he realized, were getting out of hand. He no longer felt safe! He had to act quickly and wasted no time at all when he learnt that we were joining all of you for dinner last night. Since it was again impossible to predict which cup to spike because everybody had the same drink, the poison had to be administered at the table itself, and the one person who could do that was Axel himself! He blamed James, but James was two seats away from him. It would have been impossible for him to have pulled it off without anyone noticing. You see, Axel knew there was a flaw in his plan, but he had to try anyway. He had hoped that by boldly and brazenly accusing James, he would have stopped us from looking any further, from thinking any further! But then, he makes another mistake! He very clearly states that he did not want us to report that to the police. Why? Who, in their right frame of mind, would defend the person who just tried to murder him, considering they aren't related in any way? But I don't blame Axel; he simply had no choice! He had to do all that to protect himself and not blow the problem to bigger proportions. If we had gone to the police, no doubt there would have been more questions, and either way it turns out, it wouldn't be in his favour. The first case: the police see through his lies and nullify his accusation. The second case, the less likely and more far-fetched one: James gets thrown into jail, possibly even be sentenced to death for the murder of Geraldine. No! Axel had agreed to help Agnes do Geraldine in, but he wasn't prepared to go any further. He just wanted us to close the case, with no more damage done, and to return to Hong Kong, hoping to forget his mistakes here and move on. He knew the police would accept whatever I said as final. Then, I remembered that Axel said roughly the same things as Agnes did, regarding the whole 'just-close-the-case' concept. That was when

I saw the possibility that Agnes and Axel were in it together, and everything else fell into place!"

"Why should I need Axel's help? Why should I trust him? I hardly know him. He isn't even part of the family!" said Agnes.

"Exactly! He isn't a member of this family! You realized that he, being the most neutral, was a valuable asset. You knew that we were more likely to believe him than anyone else. So, you needed him to manipulate us as the situation required. You probably paid him a token sum to help you, though I don't know how much, and also Axel, being so young, would find your proposition exciting and challenging. Besides, Axel isn't staying here for long. When he's home in Hong Kong, you, Agnes, would be as safe as could be. And why? Because this murder, as straightforward as it seems, is difficult, if not impossible, to successfully accomplish alone. It was a 'game' for two or three, constantly covering each other's tracks and playing key roles in the murder. The police couldn't see the solution, of course, because they were looking for individual murderers, not a pair. So, they failed where I succeeded. Axel was indeed of great help to you, Agnes, what with the game sheet idea and placing the poison into the cup to throw us all off! Admit it; you couldn't have succeeded without him!"

"That's crazy! What are you even saying? You have no proof whatsoever!" said Agnes angrily.

"Yes, I do! I've been doing my homework, and I learnt that strychnine kills in less than an hour, but if the poison was really in the coffee, she would have died long before the mahjong game ended. But, the three eye witnesses sitting close to her all agree that she was quite normal during the rounds. And of course, that doesn't tally with the 'facts' presented, but with what I have just suggested. I suppose, if this issue were to be pursued, the police would be convinced that the coffee didn't kill her. New evidence would surface and you have a lot of answering to do. That is proof enough indeed!"

"Enough! Enough! Agnes, we've lost," said Axel to Agnes. Then turning to face us, he said, "The only question left is what next?" His face was expressionless, almost as if he had accepted defeat. There was stone cold silence in the room as everybody tried to absorb the truth.

"What's next is not really up to us. We agreed to come in and solve this case, but we aren't under any further obligation to report this to the police. As far as the police is concerned, the case is as good as closed anyway," continued Andrew. "Agnes?"

"Ok! Ok! I did it!" said Agnes, sobbing uncontrollably. I killed her because she was a monster! A monster who killed my father, before I had even met him! Do you know what it's like to be fatherless? Do you know how difficult it was growing up never knowing the love of my father? I've hated her for as long as I could remember! I don't care about her money, I cared only about avenging my father's death! And come on, all of you know we are better off with her dead."

"What I don't understand is why you called us in the first place."

"Because I was stupid! That's why! I should have realized I couldn't escape with it, but I was so sure I couldn't fail! So sure that you'd give up, that I'd win and get away scot-free! The police's findings weren't convincing enough! I needed you to prove it was a suicide. I needed you to deal with the turmoil in the household once and for all, but not like this!" She buried her face in her palms and didn't stop crying for some time. It was as if time stood still, and nobody moved.

We left them then without saying much else, trusting that they could cope with the truth, accept it, and move on.

It was only then that I understood what achievement was, what success was, what victory was, but I never thought I should feel the way I did. What was victory, when only loss and hopelessness echoed all around? As I looked at all the despair in their faces, I wondered how Andrew could have the heart to do that sort of thing, again and again. He might have won in the eyes of justice, but he had certainly lost everything in the eyes of humanity. But I never said any of that to him; no, I just allowed it to fade away . . . .

Epilogue

It was only about three months later that we received a letter. It was from Audrey, and it read:

Dear Mr. Sommers and Tony,

I know we hardly know each other, and that fate must have been mad to plan the crossing of our paths for even those mere three days, but my husband and I feel you ought to know how things have developed in our household since what happened. Just as you so graciously left the choice to our family to decide on 'what next', we have chosen to keep you informed; not out of obligation but out of responsibility.

First up, we sold the house. It was a difficult decision, but I think you know as well we had to. I never blamed anybody for the deaths; I had always suspected the house itself. It reeked of evil and discontentment. We used a portion of the money to buy a nice little house down at Whittle Avenue, and donated the rest to a children's home. Finally, the house was of some good use.

And, yes, my husband owns his own clinic now with the money my aunt had left us, as well as half of Agnes's share. She refused her portion of the inheritance you see, insisting she would rather die than take the money, and also impressed upon us that she could no longer face us with her shame. So, she has left home, taking almost nothing with her. We tried to stop her, saying that we really had forgiven her and would never tell anybody, and that we had moved on, but no, she left anyway, to we know not where, promising to write to us if she could ever face herself or us again. I think she just wanted to start afresh, to rediscover herself, and we all keep her in our prayers and wait for her to return.

Alvin has gone back to London where he has started his own accounting firm and writes to us or calls us very frequently. I suppose he's doing very well there and we're all very happy for him. Mother is staying with us, and so is Emily who decided to stay on and help us with the housework. I'm afraid we had to let Betty and Sebastian go, but with such a small household now, there is really no need for either cook or butler. And I'm pleased to say I've taken over the cooking responsibilities of our family!

Bobby has almost forgotten the whole incident and has put it behind him, and occasionally sends e-mails to Axel, who has yet to reply to any of them. But maybe this is best for both of them. Wherever Axel may be, we hope he's fine and safe and as carefree as Bobby is. He is, after all, not a bad boy. There have been times when I've wished my own boy would be more like him! Though I do wonder exactly why Axel agreed to help her; he never did tell us his reasons, even after you left.

Anyway, Deb and Eve still come visiting often, but not for mahjong. They're into poker now. I still have the mahjong set though, so if you ever visit, we'll know what to do! Oh, right! I almost forgot; our address is 7, Whittle Avenue, Roseburn Estate. Do drop by every now and then.

Well, I've reached the end of my letter. It would be paradoxical if I were to say 'thank you', but in all good faith and manners, thank you for your help. And until we meet again, goodbye!

Love,
Audrey Tholson

P.S. : My husband wants you to be very clear that he was *not* downstairs the night my aunt died, despite what Axel may have told you. I told him that surely you will believe him, but he insisted anyway. I guess men will always be men!

THE END

About the Author

Elgin Lee, born in December 1996, hails from Penang, Malaysia and is currently a college student, studying in Selangor. He writes fiction in his free time out of passion for it and as a means of expressing himself and his creativity as a teenager.